Cry Witch

Naomi A. Hintze

Cry Witch

Random House: New York

Library of Congress Cataloging in Publication Data

Hintze, Naomi A.   Cry witch.

I. Title.
PZ4.H665Cr   [PS3558.155]   813'.5'4   74-19063
ISBN 0-394-49548-9

Manufactured in the United States of America

35798642

FIRST EDITION

Cry Witch

I

The girl in the small kitchen moved quickly, quietly, listening while she assembled cheese, crackers, and fruit on a dessert tray. Over the hiss of snow at the window, the percolating of coffee, she was trying to hear the conversation of her three guests in the other room.

In sneakers, blue jeans, and white shirt, flat-hipped, modestly endowed as to chest, she looked closer to her fourteenth birthday than to the twenty-fourth she would celebrate in June. Her hair was pale yellow, shaggy as a chrysanthemum. Her eyes were big, their color changeable as the sea. Her face was changeable too. It could have a funny-girl look, a wistful, lost, street-Arab look.

Sometimes it took on another look which Josh Lincoln,

her boss and frequent date, had told her reminded him of a saint in a medieval painting, one of those with upturned, preoccupied eyes, whose mind seemed to be on matters that had little to do with the Virgin ascending.

Her name was Virginia, although none of her co-workers at World Wide Airlines ever called her that. She had called herself Gigi since before she could talk straight.

So far, it had not been a very good party. Max and Carol, the married couple, had been sniping at each other. The four cups stacked for coffee fell to one side now with a little clatter, so that Gigi lost a sentence or two. She heard Carol say, "Josh Lincoln, I don't believe it!"

Max laughed. "Don't be so gullible, Carol. Josh is just putting you on."

Gigi appeared at the doorway of the dining alcove, and as Josh got up to take the heavy tray from her she said, "What don't you believe, Carol? I was trying to eavesdrop out there, but I seem to have missed something."

Carol, with smooth brown hair drawn back into a knot, was leaning to light her cigarette from one of the candles in the middle of the table. "Guess what—he can hypnotize people, Gee."

Gigi turned to look into Josh's bright blue eyes. "You never told me that."

Josh's face was craggy, homely, until he smiled. He was smiling now. "You never asked me."

"I'm asking now. Tell."

"Oh"—he spread his big hands—"there's not a whole lot to tell. It's been so many years ago—six, seven—that I hardly ever think about it any more. I probably couldn't do it now if I tried."

"But you're not the type, Josh." Carol looked from Max to Gigi. "Is he? Do you think he's the type, Gee?"

4

"Well, no, but . . ."

Josh moved his chair back a little to cross his long legs. He had rough dark hair. Heavy, neat black brows. A way of holding his head up and back a little, smiling a little, as if he knew you, saw right through you, and liked you anyway. His blue eyes were amused. "Describe the type. No, never mind. I should have piercing black eyes that light up with a magic power. And I should wear—a cape?"

"No, no. We're not quite that stupid. Only you seem so—so normal." Carol looked at the others for reinforcement. "The only time—the only time—I ever thought you had piercing eyes was last week at work when I told you I had let that sweet old lady give me a bum check for a ticket to Los Angeles."

"Well, she looked enough like Helen Hayes. You said that yourself. You should have known. Didn't you see *Airport*?"

"Sure, but—she showed me her grandchildren's pictures. That was when she was looking through her wallet, trying to find identification. One of the babies looked to be about Malinda's age, and we got off on babies. Are you going to have it taken out of my pay, boss?"

"No. My plan is to have you put at the end of the bag chute for six months where you'll have to use your muscles instead of your brains."

"Brains?" Max drawled the word.

"Don't get started again, you two." Gigi was pouring coffee. She liked Carol; Max, heavy-faced, handsome, was sometimes hard to take. She handed a cup of coffee to Josh. "Hypnotize me."

"Absolutely no. I wouldn't even try."

Max added cream and sugar to his coffee. "I should think you'd want this cute chick in your power. Haven't you been working on that these past months—or do I just have that kind of mind?"

"You do have that kind of mind, and I have been working on it, but I wouldn't take unfair advantage even if I could." He turned to look at Gigi.

"I trust you, boss."

"Forget it. It's not a parlor game."

"I know that." The yellow of the candle flames combined with the blue in Gigi's eyes to make them look as green as the grape she was putting in her mouth. "But do it."

"No."

"Yes. Let's hurry and finish up here so we can all go sit in front of the fire and get comfortable and you can prove whether or not you were just putting us on."

"I wasn't putting you on."

"Well, how did you learn to hypnotize? Did you send away for one of those correspondence courses I've seen advertised, or was it a natural talent?"

"It's not a talent. Anybody can learn to do it . . . Say, what kind of cheese is this? It's pretty good. Max, next time you fly to Spain, I want you to bring me back some of their goat's-milk cheese. You can *habla español* a little, can't you? I can make a Greek salad with Spanish cheese that's—"

Carol interrupted. "Don't try to change the subject. We're not letting you off the hook. Describe. Go into detail. How did you happen to get into it?"

Max said, "He found out he could con the babes into—"

"Max, please shut up. Go look at television or something. I'm interested, aren't you, Gee?"

Gigi was nodding. "Start at the beginning."

"Well, I attended a few how-to sessions in connection with a psychology course. Got interested, took a short course. That summer I made a little money helping a dentist friend in the little Ohio town near my folks' farm. Some of his patients, for one reason or another, couldn't take the Novocaine, procaine, or whatever it is dentists use. One boy, about twelve years old, had an unholy fear of the needle. And so I would just take this kid through the relaxing business—"

"Be specific."

Josh looked around the table, gave a resigned shrug. "There are lots of ways. Sometimes a pendulum or something shiny is moved back and forth in front of the patient's eyes, and you just tell him to concentrate on that. Anything bright will do if the subject keeps his eyes on it. I've seen a metronome used—the monotonous click, click seems to help some people relax and forget themselves. I just told this kid to keep his eyes on the bright light over the dentist's chair until his eyes got heavy. I told him to imagine that the sun was shining, but that he was getting too sleepy to stare at it any longer."

"Then what?" Gigi put down her coffee cup carefully so as not to cause any distracting noise.

"Well, I used this thing I'd read in a book. I'm rusty now, but it went something like, 'Imagine that you are lying very comfortably in a little boat. The waves are very pleasantly rocking you back and forth, back and forth, lulling you, helping you to relax. You are relaxing now, feeling more comfortable than you have ever felt before . . .' "

The room was very quiet. Josh leaned back in his chair, his hands clasped behind his head as he stared at the ceiling. His deep voice became a drone. "You are very comfortable now, very relaxed, very calm. In a few seconds you will hear the distant hum of a power boat starting up, coming closer, just a buzzing sound that will only deepen your feeling of being very lazy, very comfortable and relaxed, with the sun shining and your eyes closed and the waves gently rocking. And the buzzing sound will help you sink more and more deeply into this pleasant, enjoyable sensation of lazy, restful comfort."

The drone of his voice stopped. He looked around the table at the three pairs of eyes that were so intent on his. He laughed a little, and said in his normal voice, "So then the dentist would start up his drill."

Carol gave a tap to the side of her head. "Wow, you almost had me under there for a minute."

Max said, "Dirty trick, if you ask me, to sneak up on an unsuspecting kid like that."

"No, Max, not at all. The boy knew what he was there for when he sat down in the chair. I had his confidence and he really believed, for as long as it took the dentist to do the work, that it was a pleasant, relaxing experience. Hypnosis can be very useful medically."

"Then why don't they use it more?" Carol asked.

"It takes a lot longer than the usual anesthetic—sometimes three or more sessions before a patient can get accustomed to entering a deep hypnotic state. But there have been many instances of major surgery being performed under hypnosis."

Max said they'd never get him to let anybody cut anything out of him without an anesthetic.

Gigi folded her hands under her chin. "When will you hypnotize me?"

"Never." Josh put his fist against her jaw in a gentle nudge. "So never mind asking."

"Tonight. Here tonight with just the four of us. Me first, because this is my house"—she gave an explosive little giggle—"and then Carol and then Max."

Max shook his head. "No chance. Want to know what I think?"

"Not particularly, dear." Carol said it sweetly.

"I don't believe there is any such thing as hypnotism. I've seen those guys on the stage and they never fooled me for a minute. I don't see how it is possible to—"

"Neither do I," Josh said, his tone mild, "but I have to accept a lot of things I don't understand, that nobody understands. Take the learning process. Nobody understands it. I read a piece in a magazine recently—*Time*, I think—that said there is no known basis for learning, that, *logically*, it is impossible for it to happen. And yet we know that it does. Memory, that whole ball of wax, is a fascinating mystery. Our conscious minds remember only a fractional part of all the experiences we've ever had. Most of the stuff would be a nuisance to have to remember, some of it junk, some of it memories we've suppressed, and yet it's all there, like on a computer, buried in the subconscious."

Gigi said thoughtfully, "And what we are now may be, to some extent, influenced by what our conscious minds have forgotten. Right, Josh?"

"Right."

"The whole subject fascinates me. Somewhere I've read —maybe in that same piece you mentioned, Josh—about a neurosurgeon who was operating on a woman's brain under local anesthetic. When he touched a certain part of her brain with an electrode, she recalled a song she thought she had forgotten."

"Oh, my God," said Max, "what good does it do anybody to remember an old song? I don't want anybody fooling around in my brain, just for kicks, with an electrode. And as for hypnosis, I've got too much of a will of my own ever to let anybody put me through any of those monkeyshines."

Josh said quickly, "You'd be hard to do, maybe impossible. I'd never try it on you."

"Also"—Carol's voice was sweet again—"haven't I heard that it takes an average or better intelligence?"

"It does." Josh grinned at Max. "There's nothing wrong with your intelligence, buddy, or they'd never let you fly a plane. But hypnosis is a consent state. The subject has to allow himself to accept suggestions, has to want, for whatever reason, to be hypnotized."

Gigi touched her forehead and bowed. "O Master, you see before you the perfect subject. I am suggestible. I am a true believer. And I have a reason."

"What's the reason?"

Her pale eyes met his bright blue ones for a moment, then she got up and started clearing the table. "Intellectual curiosity, let's say. Or morbid fascination with what goes on inside my head."

Josh picked up dishes and followed her to the kitchen to help clean up while Carol went to call the baby-sitter and Max looked at the Globetrotters on TV. Josh said, "Tell me your real reason, baby, for wanting me to hypnotize you."

Gigi rinsed the plates, put them in the dishwasher. "Did you ever try to regress anyone?"

"Yes."

"How hard is it to do?"

"Depends."

"On what?"

"On the subject, mostly. The depth of hypnosis that's reached. There are different stages, and the subject has to go into a deep somnambulistic state to achieve a real age regression. Or are you wanting to get back to another life? I bet you think you were once a temple dancer."

"I *was* a temple dancer. How'd you guess?" She crossed her eyes, put her arms over her head, and moved her flat stomach provocatively, then broke off the little exhibition with a high, gay laugh. "No. I'm not sure I buy all that stuff, but I do go along with what you were saying at the table about all the memories that are buried. Are you really convinced that they can be—well, tapped under hypnosis?"

"I've seen it done. I saw a fifty-ish woman, gray-haired and wrinkled, taken back through the years to when she was a coquettish young girl, and then a little child, crying over the death of a kitten. She was taken all the way back to the birth process. It was scary—she had breathing problems. Thank heaven, it wasn't my show."

"I don't want to go back that far. I just want to be taken back to my early childhood. There are some things I've got to find out."

"For instance . . ."

"I'm curious about my mother. I can't remember her. She died—I've told you—before I was three."

"I'm curious about you." He put his arms about her and looked into her eyes. "On the job, you're great, you come on with that million-dollar public-relations smile. You charm the customers with that funny laugh of yours. Sometimes when we're alone your face gets that saint look, with something else behind it that makes me think I'm getting somewhere. And then you put me off by clowning it up."

"Poor baby." She kissed him, a fast peck, and would have pulled away.

His arms tightened. "There you go, always putting me on 'hold.' Why I haven't hung up on you long before this—"

"You like me." She put her fingers at the corners of his mouth as if to make him smile.

"Cut it out. I'm sick of like."

"And I like you. I like squares now."

"Thanks."

Her laugh was high, infectious. "I used to like guys with beads and ponytails and sandals and one earring—"

His hand went over her mouth. "Sometime I hope to be able to finish all of what I've got to say. You're always kissing me and then ducking away like some kid playing post office. I try to talk to you seriously about us and you change the subject."

Gigi turned her face away. "Give me time, Josh."

"It's been weeks, months. How much time?"

Her moon-child eyes met his. She whispered, "Maybe not very much more."

He bent his head, his lips closing on hers. She kissed him back, relaxed against him, letting him draw her close. And then she moved her head. She said, with her lips against his cheek, "I like you so much. You are my very, very best friend. Please hypnotize me, Josh Lincoln."

He tilted his head back to look at her. "If I thought I could find out what goes on inside your head . . . Okay, I'll hypnotize you. Anyhow, try."

Gigi started the dishwasher and they went into the living room.

Carol slammed up the telephone. "It took me all this time to get that miserable baby-sitter! I was about to call the operator to ask if the phone was off the hook. I figured the boyfriend was there, and she just didn't want to be disturbed."

Gigi smiled. "Don't you remember when you were a teenager?"

Max said, "That's her trouble. She remembers too well."

Josh put a log on the fire. "Okay, troops. We are going to have a little session. Turn off the tube, Max. You can find out who won on the eleven o'clock news."

Reluctantly, Max turned off the TV set. "You two, out there in the kitchen talking—I think you've got something cooked up."

Carol said, "One skeptic can ruin the whole thing, Max."

Josh disregarded them. "Where would you like to sit, Gee?"

"Where do you want me? Should I just sit, lie down, or what?"

"It doesn't matter. How about that tan chair with the footstool? I just want you to be in a completely relaxed position. Put your feet up, lean your head back."

Gigi tucked a pillow behind her and sprawled, her long legs extended onto the footstool.

Carol said uneasily, "Wait a minute. What happens if you can't wake her up?"

Josh turned off all the lights except for the one behind Gigi. From the dining alcove, he brought a straight chair and positioned it in front of her. "No problem. Once, I'll admit, I did see a man get into such a pleasant, relaxed state that he didn't want to leave it. So he was just allowed to sleep it off. Okay, Gigi? You're not worried about anything, are you?"

She flopped her shaggy head sideways as if she were already asleep.

Josh reached to touch her head. "Listen, darlin', let's not clown—all right? Just this once. We're not going to get anywhere at all if you're not going to be perfectly serious."

"I'm sorry. That was silly. I really am perfectly serious about this whole thing."

"Okay, then." He sat on the chair in front of her. "Just one thing before we start, is there anything you'd like to have me avoid, any period in your life that you'd rather not talk about?"

Her eyes met his, very sober now. "Yes. The year of nineteen seventy-two, when I was twenty-two. That was kind of a bad year."

"Okay. Anything else?"

"No."

"How far back would you like to go?"

"Back to when I was about two and a half, December, when my mother was alive. We were in—"

"Never mind. Don't tell me anything else right now. We'll just see what we can find out."

2

T*he* room was very quiet. Behind the closed kitchen door they could hear the sounds made by the dishwasher. The fire crackled, whispered a little. The snow, turning to sleet, made a soft sibilance against the windows. Max and Carol sat on the sofa, and Josh sat facing Gigi. "Comfortable?"

"Yep. One thing, Josh. No tricks. I don't want to waste time doing silly things like—"

"No tricks. You have my promise that you are not going to do anything that is in any way embarrassing or just for laughs. I want you to have complete confidence in me."

"I do."

"Fine. I just want you to relax. You are going to have a

15

pleasant experience. All right?" His blue eyes were calm, very serious.

"All right." She gave him a little smile, put her hands on the arms of the chair.

"Comfortable?"

"Very."

"Take a deep breath. Good. Another. Very good. Now—" He leaned to hold his big hand close to her forehead, just above her eyes so that she had to look up.

"What am I supposed to do now?"

"Just watch my hand as I bring it down. Keep your eyes on my hand. As my hand descends slowly, slowly, your eyes are watching, your lids are lowering. And you are very comfortable, very relaxed, no tensions at all, no apprehensions, as you feel your lids getting heavy, heavier. Your eyes are closing now as I bring my hand down so slowly in front of your face, down now under your chin."

The droning, confident sound of his voice stopped for a moment as he leaned back away from her. Her mascaraed lashes were fanned against her cheeks. "It is a very pleasant feeling to sit there with your eyes closed."

"Very . . . pleasant." She spoke softly.

"You are relaxing now from the tips of your toes. Feel your toes relax. Your ankle bones. All tension is gone, gone. The feeling of complete relaxation moves up your legs now to your calves, to your knees. A pleasant, good feeling. Now up to your thighs, with each muscle, each bone relaxing as the pleasant feeling steals around through your backbone, each vertebra relaxing. This feeling of relaxation moves through your stomach, up into your lungs as you breathe slowly, deeply. A pleasant, good feeling of wellbeing. Your neck is relaxing. The muscles of your face, right up to your scalp, to the top of your head, are letting go. Very good. You are loose, relaxed, with no tensions, no anxieties."

Out in the kitchen the dishwasher changed cycles, began a long, humming roar. Josh said, "Each sound you hear only deepens your state of relaxation, so that you hear nothing but the sound of my voice. I want you to tell me your name now, your full name."

"Gigi—Virginia. Virginia Ann Lang." Her voice was almost a whisper, steady.

"Fine. Very good. What is the date today?"

"January the sixteenth."

"And the year?"

"Nineteen seventy-four."

"How old are you?"

"I'll be twenty-four in June."

"So you were born in nineteen-fifty?"

"Yes."

"Good. That makes for easy arithmetic. All right now, we are going to count backward from twenty to one. And as we count backward, I am going to ask you to imagine that you are descending on an escalator, down, down, with no effort involved, into the depths of your subconscious. Twenty . . . nineteen . . . eighteen. Your hand rests on the railing as you float securely, safely downward. Seventeen . . . sixteen . . . fifteen. And with each count you are deepening your state of relaxation, letting go, so comfortably, so effortlessly, so safely. Fourteen . . . thirteen . . . twelve . . . eleven . . ."

Gigi was breathing slowly, deeply, with no flickering of the heavy lashes.

". . . four, three, two, one. Very good. You are so relaxed now, so comfortable. I want you to imagine that a string is attached to your right wrist. At the other end of the string is a balloon filled with helium, lighter than air. It tugs gently at your wrist. Very gently, so that you feel it lifting your wrist, your hand. No effort involved. You cannot keep it from rising gently, steadily, all by itself. Feel it, the steady tug on your wrist. It is rising, rising . . ."

Gigi's right wrist quivered, moved upward a few inches, fell back.

"Very good. Fine. It is January the sixteenth, nineteen seventy-four. Now I want you to go back, back in time. You want to go back in time. We will go back just a little to last summer, the summer of nineteen seventy-three. Can you tell me about a time during that summer that is pleasant to remember, when you were relaxed and happy?"

"Yes. I am in Washington. I have a job, a new job." Gigi's voice was sleepy and the words came slowly. "I will start working in July for World Wide Airlines at Dulles Airport. I will have travel benefits."

"That's good. Okay, we are going to go back now to another summer. You are getting younger. You are going back, back to nineteen sixty-six. How old are you?"

"Sixteen."

"Where are you now in the summer of nineteen sixty-six?"

"Peoria. Peoria, Illinois."

"You live in Peoria, Illinois. And you are sixteen. Can you tell me about a time, a happy time, in the summer of nineteen sixty-six?"

"Mmm—yes. I am in the woods with my boyfriend. We are walking across the stones in a brook. A hike with— But we are alone now."

"What is your boyfriend's name?"

"It is Freddy. Freddy Palmer. He is older than me. He is going to college soon." She gave a breathless little laugh and said rapidly, "I am falling—falling into the brook. He tries to catch me, but I fall. I am soaked, wet all over. My hair . . . it is so long . . . and it's all wet. We are laughing. He kisses me, my face all wet. My dress is soaked and he says—Freddy—that I should take it off and hang it on a hickory limb. He says that's what you do. But I don't want to take off my dress. No, I won't do that. He thinks I am funny. But he kisses me some more. And then his hands . . . That is all. I am too young. It is nice, but . . . That's all."

"That's all. Very good. We will go back to another time. You are getting younger, younger. Nineteen sixty-five, sixty-four, sixty-three. Stop me when you want to tell about another happy time."

Her face clouded, eyes closed, as she shook her head. "Nothing. I can't remember any time when—"

"How about a Christmas? Say, when you were eight. It is Christmas, nineteen fifty-eight. Can you tell me about Christmas day when you were eight—eight and a half years old? Did you get presents?"

"Yes. A terrarium. I got a terrarium. And a microscope and books. You know, like that."

"Who gave them to you? Santa Claus?"

"No, no." She gave a little giggle. "I don't believe in Santa Claus any more. I am too old. That's silly. Grandfather gave them to me."

"Where do you live?"

"Right here. Right here in Peoria."

Josh glanced around toward Max and Carol on the sofa. "Right here in Peoria. Do you live with your grandfather now?"

"Yes."

"Who else lives in your house?"

"Nobody. Just the housekeeper."

"I see. What happened today?"

"I went to his study this morning."

"Oh? Did you take your grandfather a present?"

"Yes. Sure. A pretty tie. I picked it out all by myself. I saved my allowance. It is yellow and red because all his ties are dark—black and dark. And some shaving lotion—that's what else I gave him. And something . . . I forgot. Oh, a box of candy with cherries in the middle because that's my favorite. Chocolate with cherries and it runs down your chin."

"Was he happy with his presents?"

She shrugged. "Yes, I guess so. He said, 'Thank you, Virginia.' Nobody else gives him presents."

"I see. Yes, well, what else? Did you have a big Christ-mas dinner with turkey?"

Another shrug. "Yes. We went to the club. They had a big Christmas tree in the middle."

"Did you like the tree?"

"It wasn't our tree. It was everybody's tree."

"Oh. Well, all right, Gigi." Josh glanced at his watch. "Now we are going to go back, back. It is Christmas time again, the week between Christmas and New Year's. You are just a little girl. It is nineteen fifty-two. You are two and a half years old now, Gigi. Do you want to talk about that?"

"We had stockings."

"New stockings? Did you put them on?" An adult, teasing a little child.

"No, no!" She giggled like a little girl, cupping her hand over her mouth. "Wif pwesents in. Pwesents in the stockings. That's how you do." Her eyes were half open now. She twisted in her chair, pointed her toes. "You hang up your stockings, an' . . . an' . . . he comes. Santa Claus comes."

"Did you see Santa Claus?"

"No, no, I am sleeping." She said some words in another language. Josh looked around at Max. Max nodded, whispered, "Spanish."

"How old are you now?"

She held up two fingers. "But I am almost fwee. Soon. Almost."

"In June you will be three. Well, that's not too long to wait. Where are you now?"

"At Mimi's house. It is big, big—" She spread her arms wide. "I could get lost." Solemnly, she nodded her head. "Yes. Mommy says that. An' Mimi lives there. An' Catalina, an'—"

"Who is Mimi?"

Gigi cocked her head to one side, frowning a little. "Don't you know who Mimi is?"

"No. Who is Mimi?"

"Just Mimi, that's who she is. My mommy's mommy."

"Oh, I see. And who is Catalina?"

"Catalina is—Catalina. She helps me take my baf."

"Your bath?"

"Sí. Baño. Catalina is *muy amable*."

"Do you speak Spanish?"

"Sí. *Hablo español*. Sometimes."

"Good for you. Uh—well, tell me some more. Did you get some nice presents for Christmas?"

"Sí." She nodded. "*Muchos regalos*. And everybody is laughing, laughing. And everybody sings songs around the Cwistmas twee. An' I got a wed dwess. An' my mommy, she tied a wed wibbon on my hair. An' . . . an' . . . you want to know what else?"

"I want to know what else."

"I got a dolly. It can say, 'Mama—Mama—' like that. An' you want to know what else it can do?"

"What else can it do?"

"It wets. That's what it does, it wets its panties." She cupped her hand over her mouth, giggling. "But I don't. I am big. I don't wet my panties any, any more. Hardly ever. An' I don't have to take my nap. Much. Because I am big. Sometimes, though, I go to my bed an' I look at my books and sometimes—sometimes I take a nap. An' then my mommy comes an' . . . an' . . ."

For a moment Gigi's face had the look of a sleepy child just wakening from a nap. And then her expression changed. It became bewildered and then apprehensive. She had been lying back in the chair, but now she sat up straight.

"Mommy!" The cry was sharp. Her eyes were round, fixed, as she seemed to stare at another scene. Her mouth turned down. Tears. She dug her eyes with her fists. She said, half sobbing, her mouth puckering, "*Mama—tengo miedo* . . ."

Josh glanced around at Max. He translated, frowning a little as if not quite sure, "I am afraid . . . ?"

A torrent of excited Spanish. Josh put his hand on Gigi's, but she shook him off and reached her arms beyond him. Terror in her eyes, she screamed, a chilling sound in the quiet room:

"Witch, witch! Mommy, Mommy! No, no!"

3

Josh knelt quickly and caught the hysterical girl in his arms. "Gigi! Gigi! You are safe, darling. Everything is all right. I am holding you. Nothing can hurt you. You are safe, safe. There is nothing here to be afraid of."

She stared at him as if she had never seen him before, her wet eyes glassy. "Mama . . . ?"

"Gigi—honey—it's me, Josh."

Her breathing was ragged. She blinked, shook her head, and then hid her face on his chest.

He held her close and spoke rapidly. "We are going to count forward now. Very fast, we are going to count up through the years. You are no longer a little child. You are getting older. It is nineteen fifty-three, fifty-four, fifty-five.

You are five years old. It is nineteen sixty, and you are ten, growing older. And now it is nineteen sixty-five, sixty-six, sixty-seven. And now, right now, it is January sixteenth, nineteen seventy-four, and you are grown up now, almost twenty-four years old. You are here in your own house. Max and Carol are with us and I am holding you safely in my arms."

Gigi's eyes had closed. She was relaxing in his arms; the sobbing had subsided and her breathing was beginning to be more regular.

"In a moment now I am going to be saying, one . . . two . . . three . . . and you are going to open your eyes, feeling relaxed and perfectly fine, with no memories that will worry you. One . . . two . . . three . . ."

Gigi opened her eyes. She drew a deep, shaky breath and looked up at Josh, puzzled, dazed. She wiped the tears from her cheeks, looked at her wet fingers, smeared with mascara. "What happened? What did I do?"

Josh moved back a little. He glanced at Max and Carol, who had come to their feet. Carol spread her hands. "Good lord, Gee, you surely must—"

Gigi looked from one face to another. "I—I half remember that something bad was happening."

Josh reached for her hands again. "You're okay now. But you seemed to be reliving a very frightening experience."

Max said, "All I know, it scared the livin' be-jasus out of me when you screamed like that."

"Me too," said Josh. "Gigi, look. I got over my head, girl. I should never have tried to do this. I'm just an amateur. I haven't had enough experience to know how to cope when these things happen."

"But, Josh, I have only the vaguest . . . What do you think frightened me?"

"I don't know. In the first place—and this was my mistake, I suppose—I should have given you the prehypnotic suggestion that you would remember. Quite often the ability to recall is impaired by a shock. Many times hypnotism is able to set aside that block—"

Carol said, "But a kid who's only two and a half years old would hardly remember anything anyhow."

"Under hypnosis a person is sometimes able to go a lot further back than that. Gigi, it seems obvious that you have some subliminal memory of a very traumatic experience."

"I know."

"You *know*? How?"

"I have been hypnotized before."

Josh got up, ran his hands through his dark hair. "Oh, Gigi, *now* you tell me. I should have guessed, though, when you went under so easily. People don't usually go into it that fast unless they're hypersuggestible."

"I think I am."

"How many times have you been hypnotized?"

"I'm not sure—several times. We used to do it at school."

"And the more times you're hypnotized, the easier it is."

"But I have been regressed only once before."

"When was that?"

"Last summer. It was—well, the kind of thing you don't approve of. A parlor-game sort of thing. Last July, just before I started working, a bunch of us were at the beach. And this guy . . . Well, anyhow, I was hypnotized and regressed and I went into this screaming, crying thing. I was afraid you wouldn't do it if I told you."

"Right." His tone was fervent. "I certainly wouldn't have

done it if I had known you wanted to get back to some childhood experience that scared you half to death. I'm not equipped to handle anything as heavy as that. Only an expert should risk it—I mean, a real hypnoanalyst."

"What did I say?"

There was a silence. Max had walked over to the window to look out at the snow. Carol said, "Oh, tell her, Josh. What's the harm? Maybe it's something the kid needs to know."

"I need to know."

He said cautiously, "You said—screamed, really—something about a witch."

"Can you remember the exact words that I said?"

"Yes. There weren't that many of them. Your exact words were, 'Witch, witch! Mommy, Mommy! No, no!'"

Gigi nodded her blond head slowly. "Yes, yes. That's right. That's what I did that other time—they told me I said just about those same words."

Josh came back to sit in front of her again. "But what did it mean? Do you have any clue?"

"No. Not from memory. Just from the few things I have been told. Did I say anything in Spanish? They told me I did that the other time."

"Yes. I didn't know you could speak Spanish."

"I can't, really. Took it in college, so that I know a few words. But when I was little—you know how little kids pick up a language easily—apparently I spoke it fairly well. Both times under hypnosis, tonight and that other time, I've been told I spoke Spanish. I seemed to be remembering something that happened on the island of Majorca."

Carol said, "I didn't know you ever lived there. But then, there's a lot about you that I don't know."

"I never actually lived there. My mother took me for a

visit of several months to Mimi's house—she's my grand-mother—before I was three. And then, during the week between Christmas and New Year's—"

Carol said, "Christmas! Yes, that's something you men-tioned. You said something about a 'Cwistmas twee.' Hon-estly, I had goose bumps. It was fantastic, seeing you turn into a little girl again."

Josh said, "Gigi, during that week between Christmas and New Year's—do you know what happened?"

"My mother died."

"How?" asked Carol.

Gigi combed the fringe of the pillow she was holding, separating the strands with her fingers.

"Was it wrong for me to ask that? I'm sorry. Maybe you'd rather not talk about it."

Gigi lifted her shoulders. "I don't mind talking about it, I guess. Although it's not a thing I usually talk about. It was . . . the whole thing . . . pretty bad."

Josh said, "Skip it if you'd rather."

"No. One of those things. She took her own life." Her eyes took on their faraway, detached look, her face a blank-ness. "My mother just . . . Well, she jumped from the little balcony outside our room. We were in kind of a tower room. There were rocks below. I've never been back, but I've seen pictures of the whole place, that tower."

Carol said, "Why did she do it?"

"Carol, for God's sake!" Max's voice was angry. "Why do you have to be so nosy?"

Josh intervened. "Okay, Gigi. Listen, sweetie, you don't have to talk about it if it bothers you."

"No. It doesn't bother me so much any more. It did when I first found out. I must have been about nine when I first found out. I couldn't understand how my mother could want to"—her hands made a gesture of helplessness—"to leave me. But I guess I understand now. My father had died the year before, in an accident. Apparently she just couldn't get over it."

Josh said, "I hate the idea of probing like this, Gee, but if you really don't mind talking about it, do you suppose there is a chance that you may have witnessed your mother's death? Don't you think that it is likely that that is the traumatic experience to which you've returned both times under hypnosis?"

"I suppose so. I have been told that I had been put in my crib in the room that we shared, for my nap. I am sure that if I had witnessed anything—that if I had wakened and seen my mother about to throw herself over the railing—I would have screamed, 'Mommy, Mommy! No, no!' But the part about the witch . . ."

"Isn't there anybody you can ask? Is your grandmother still alive?"

"Very much so. She still lives in Majorca. Comes over every year or so, but she had already come and gone last summer before we did the age-regression thing at the beach."

Max said, "Here's a thought. Somebody could have come into your room, somebody dressed all in black. I've noticed that women in Spain seem to wear a lot of black. You could have thought—whoever it was—that she looked like a witch."

"Right." Carol said, "Maybe your grandmother . . . Does she look anything like a witch?"

Gigi's laughter pealed. "Anything but! Mimi is the prettiest, youngest-looking grandmother you ever saw. She's had her face lifted. She keeps her hair sort of flame-colored, no, paler than that, more apricot. She's so gay and funny, and when she comes next time I want you all to be sure to meet her. She may bewitch you, but she's no witch."

Max said, "Well, anyhow, what does a little kid that age know about witches?"

"Plenty," said Carol. "Fairy tales are full of witches. Honestly, the scary things in children's stories are enough to give any kid the heebie-jeebies. Maybe you had been looking at a book with pictures of a witch—I'm not going to let Malinda have any of them—and you had a nightmare, so when you woke up and saw this woman, maybe only a servant—"

"No, no. You're on the wrong track. Nobody was in that room except my mother and me."

Josh said, "How can you be sure? Look, darlin', the only reason I'm pursuing this line of thought is because I think you need to believe that your mother didn't commit suicide."

"I do. I'd give anything to believe that. And there's no way. Years ago, I asked Mimi. She's not the sort of person who likes to dwell on—or even admit—unpleasant things. The one time I ever got her to talk about it, she told me exactly what happened. I had been put in bed for my nap, and my mother was up there with me. There were a few guests playing bridge. That night there was to be a big dinner party, and all the servants were in this sort of courtyard preparing vegetables and that sort of thing underneath the tower room my mother and I had. Everybody was accounted for—I mean, they were all looking at each other when they heard her scream. Except for my grandmother's lover, and—"

"Your grandmother's lover?" Carol's eyes were wide.

"Oh, I've a very glamorous, very jet-set type of grandmother. And he was down on the beach, crabbing or something. When he heard her scream he came running—he was the first one to get to her. They all looked out and saw him. Every single person in that house had an absolutely perfect alibi."

"An intruder," said Max.

"No. Her door was locked from the inside when they ran up there."

"Somebody went out the window."

Gigi said wanly, "I've seen the pictures of the house. No vines on the tower. No big trees nearby. No windows, except at the top. The police came and investigated everything. The American government—a consul or somebody—got involved. And they all said that it had to be suicide."

Soothingly, Josh said, "Okay. So you've sold me. I think you probably did just have a nightmare about witches. As Carol said, kids' stories are enough to give any little girl a nightmare. Just one other thing, and then we'll let it go. I wonder if you were questioned."

"I don't know. I suppose so. But maybe not very much. Mimi told me I went into shock. I would just stare, she said, as if my mind had gone. She sent me back to my grandfather—they were divorced—and my mother and I had been living with him in Peoria. Catalina, a girl from the village who had been acting as my nursemaid, came with me and stayed for a while." She lifted her hands, palms up. "So that's it. That's every single thing I know."

Carol nodded. "You will probably never know any more. I don't see how there could be any way of probing back into a dream, and it sounds like that was what it was, more than twenty years ago. I mean, Freud or no Freud, there's no way of understanding dreams. Take the one I had last night. I dreamed that Malinda had crab grass growing out of her head, and I kept trying to comb it and—"

"And if you get started on your dumb dreams, we'll never get out of here." Max had gone to take another look out the window. "That stuff is still coming down. We've got snow tires, but if it gets much deeper, we'll never make it. What about you, Josh?"

"I've got chains on my VW. I'll stay on for a while."

Carol had started putting on her coat and boots. "Don't think it hasn't been a fascinating evening. I could stay half the night. I'm really awfully interested in stuff like this. I think we ought to get together soon again and see what—"

"No chance." Josh shook his head.

"Well, I've got this marvelous book about witchcraft around the world. Europe, you know, had thousands of witches at one time, and I'm sure Spain was one of the countries that was crawling with them. I'll bring it to you at work on Monday, Gigi."

"At work"—Josh's voice was firm—"let's not say anything about this session to anybody."

"Okay, boss. It beats the usual scuttlebutt, but if you say don't, I won't. I know which side my bread is buttered—"

"Glad you do. And if I hear yak about it, I'll know who started it and I'll put you on baggage for ten years. Angel."

"Better an angel than a witch—that's what I always say, or will say from now on. But not at work, O King." She thumbed her nose at him. "See you in the morning. Thanks, Gee. I probably won't sleep, but I hope you do."

4

Josh stood at the window, watching Max and Carol go down the sloping, twisting lane that led to the highway. He turned, giving a jerk to close the heavy draperies against the drafts that came in around the many-paned window. "Why do you have to live way the hell and gone out here with a driveway like that? The main house is so far away that you can't even see the lights."

"That's only because of the snow and trees." Also because the people who had rented her this little guest house had gone to Florida, but she didn't tell him that.

"You could have a prowler out here and scream your head off and nobody would ever hear you."

"Didn't I ever tell you I had a course in karate? Fact.

Went to the Y two nights a week for two months when I first moved to the big city. Nobody's attacked me yet, worse luck, so I've never had a chance to use my skills."

"There are other reasons why it's senseless to live out here. That driveway is so drifted now that if we get two more inches of snow, you'll never make it Monday morning. I think I'll spend the night."

Gigi had gone to the kitchen to put some things away. She called, "I think you won't. Let's not go into that again, okay? Want some more coffee?"

"Not really. Is there any left?"

"About one skimpy cup apiece. I'm heating it up."

She brought the coffee in pale pottery mugs that were about the color of her hair. Josh was adding a couple of logs to the fire, poking them to get them to settle into place.

"I'm glad you stayed, Josh. I need to talk about this for a little bit more if that's all right with you."

"I wish you would."

"We have known each other . . . how long? When did they bring you from Cleveland to be supervisor at World Wide?"

"October the first. And as much as I've seen of you, I know very little more about you than I did that first day. Until tonight."

She swirled the coffee in her cup. "Hypnotize me again and you can probably find out some more. I don't mean tonight, but—"

"Nope. Wouldn't dream of it. I can't cope. I've not had enough training. What you need is a disinterested person. I'm too interested."

"I don't want a disinterested person. I want you. Somebody who would hold me the way you did and keep me from being so frightened."

"You feel that you need to get back to this experience that frightened you so much?"

"No, no. That's not what I want. The business about the witch—I think that probably isn't important. What I want to do now is to get back past that. What I need is to feel that my mother really loved me, in spite of the fact that she chose to leave me. Oh, my grandmother has told me she did. What else would you tell a person—that your mother didn't care a hill of beans about you?"

"Oh, surely she must have loved you. I think you have to try to believe that."

"I want to believe that! I have an obsessive need to be sure of it. I think I would be all right if I could think it was true. That's why I want to be regressed. Again, Josh. To be taken back with the prehypnotic suggestion that I would remember everything that went on. But I want to by-pass that thing you saw me go into tonight."

"Probably you should not by-pass it. I think perhaps you have to remember it, to accept it. It might help you to understand."

"But it's love I want, my mother's love, not some frightening—"

"I know. But you are aware now that some bad thing did happen. And you can't go on, knowing it's there, and not finding out what it was, why it's there. Maybe it was only a bad dream. Okay. Let some skilled person take you back through that. And then I think perhaps you will be able to get back to the love."

A long moment passed before her eyes came to his and looked deeply. "Unless I can get back to that love, I don't think I will ever be able to get on to any other love."

He sighed, shaking his head.

"Haven't you ever wondered about me?"

"Haven't I."

"Wondered why I have hang-ups?"

"I don't worry about the hang-ups too much. Everybody has hang-ups. I love you, Gee."

"But you shouldn't. A nice guy like you shouldn't love a girl like me. You've told me about your family on that farm in Ohio. About your father, how strong he is, how good, how much you respect him. About your mother and her dahlias—developing, propagating, whatever it is she does to win all those prizes. I'm not the kind of girl they would want their son to marry."

"The Disney people would have to cut a lot of episodes to make a movie out of my life, honey child."

She moved away from him, went to stand at the mantel, her head lifted. For a long moment there was about her such motionless perfection of pose and slender figure that she could have been a mannequin, placed just so until such time as somebody picked her up and put her over his shoulder to carry her away.

Then she sighed, set her cup on the mantel, positioning it with a careful forefinger. "A child can survive without both parents. If he has one who loves him, one strong, responsible parent who gives him security, the feeling of being loved, he is all right. But if he does not have one parent—or one person—in his life who gives him that feeling, the child dies."

She stopped his quick protest. "I don't mean physically, but emotionally. I read that in a book that was written by a well-known child psychologist."

"You do not, surely, believe everything you read."

She faced him, the lights in the room reflected in her small gold-button earrings. "I don't. But I believe that. I am the classic case. I died—anyway, started to die—before I was three."

He began to say something, but she interrupted him again. "It's true. I have tried to prove to myself that I was not dead. Men, love—whatever that is—a couple of times. No, more than a couple of times, since I am trying to be honest with you. I had a whole year of that, the bad year that I asked you to by-pass."

"Like I said, my life—"

"Girls are different, and people who say they're not are just out of their heads. A girl gets so she doesn't like herself very much. Anyhow, that's how it was with me."

Josh slouched in his chair, stuck his big feet in chukka boots out in front of him. "That's quite a lot to throw at me without a bit more filling in."

"I'll fill in. I'll start at the beginning. My parents were married while they were both students at the University of Chicago. I suppose I was an accident."

"Does that matter? Or are you just collecting things to feel bad about?"

"Hush. Let me tell it. You can do all the analyzing you want to do later. I imagine they liked me well enough after they got me. I was kind of adorable."

"If you say so."

She stuck out her tongue, gave him a brief grin. "No, I seem not to have been too repulsive a baby. I have a photographic record of my first several months, since my father apparently was something of a camera buff. There are all the usual cliché pictures. Me in the hospital nursery—not anything you'd want to take home, with forceps marks showing. Me being brought home, though. Me in the bathinette, with a wisp of hair caught in a bow. My mother was in most of them, looking happy, very pretty. My father was in some of them. She must have taken those, because they were out of focus or the tops of heads were missing, or something. All those pictures were pasted on the first few pages of this big baby book with captions as to date, age, and so on, up to the time I was about ten months old. But after those first few pages, all the rest of the book is blank."

"That, I suppose, is when he died?"

"Yes. He was killed in a car wreck coming home from classes. So my mother—I am sure she was dazed—took me back to the family home in Peoria. She and my father had been getting by mostly on some sort of GI Bill, and there wasn't much money."

"It was good she had a place to go."

"Yes. Also no. My grandmother, Mimi—she has never let me call her anything else—was getting ready to leave Grandfather. He was in the chemistry department at the university there. Nearly twenty years older than she was—a good, high-minded, stuffy old party. She was fed to the eyeballs with him—some of this I'm kind of guessing at—but I can't imagine her ever fitting into the academic life, faculty teas and receptions, and all that. The summer before, she had gone to Europe alone, and I guess she had a high old time—young lovers, or so Grandfather indicated to me once in his tight-lipped way. She had her own money. Her father, a German immigrant, had made it big with a distillery, and that kind of money was something of an embarrassment to my teetotaling grandfather. You get the picture?"

"Yeah. Fuzzy, and a few holes, but—"

"There are a few holes for me because I know only what I've been told or surmised. Anyhow, that's where we landed, my mother and I, in that big, gloomy brick house on the bluff. God knows I remember that house. Mimi left shortly after, and her picture, so to speak, was turned to the wall. I doubt if Grandfather was much help to my mother in her grief. I am sure my laughing or crying or whatever noise I was making then must have driven him half crazy. I don't know whose side my mother was on, if anybody's, but when Mimi, a year or so later, invited the two of us to come to Majorca for the fall and winter, we went. She had bought a house there for very little money, but it was very grand. Ca'n Cornitx."

"Say that again. Spell it."

"Corn-each." She spelled it. "I don't understand about the apostrophe, but I think Ca'n means house, and I guess Cornitx is Moorish. Somebody told me once it means cliffs, or rocks."

"The Moors, if I remember, conquered—"

"Yes. And then the Spaniards got it back. The house she bought was Moorish; anyhow, begun when they were still there in the twelfth century. It has walls three and four feet thick, so she's told me. Lots of rooms on different levels wandering up along the top of this cliff that drops to the sea. Picture-book stuff. Romantic. Falling down, no bathrooms, no electricity when she bought it, but she started fixing it up. Maybe she was feeling guilty about having left my mother at her time of need, although I'm not sure Mimi ever felt guilty about anything. But she invited us and we went."

"I don't suppose you have any recollection at all of that time in your life."

"None. I have a few of the pictures Mimi gave me. Of the house, of me and my mother. In most of them, my mother is smiling, laughing, but I guess you always put on a happy face when your picture is being taken."

"Usually."

"Josh, I have studied those pictures to see if I could find out anything by the expression on her face, especially in those with me. She had hold of my hand, or she had me on her shoulders in the water, or . . . oh, I'm stringing this out too much, but it became an obsession with me, this need to know how my mother really felt about me."

"I can understand that."

"Good. Well—then she died. I've told you as much as I know about that. I was whisked away, as I've said, with Catalina to take care of me in Grandfather's house. He was my legal guardian. Catalina stayed for only a few months, but I have two or three rather vivid recollections of her. She wore a little gold cross on a chain around her neck. I used to sit on her lap and play with the cross. There was a song she used to sing to me—something about my toes. I remember the way she would take hold of them, one by one. A Spanish version, I suppose, of 'This little piggy went to market.' "

"And then she left you. Any special reason that you know of?"

"Oh, it was a different culture. She had never learned the language. She must have been awfully homesick for Majorca in that big, cold brick house. I don't wonder that she left. I do remember that she cried, and I suppose I did too. She sent me a Christmas card once with saints on it. I kept it for a long time."

"Were there ever any letters?"

"When I learned to write, I wrote her a letter. She never answered. I'm not even sure she could write Spanish. She got married, I'm sure, had kids of her own. I don't even know her last name. But Catalina is my warmest, dearest, earliest memory—the only memory that is warm and dear.

There was a succession of other people who took care of me, but there was never anybody else who really . . ."

He got up and touched her shoulder. "My poor baby. I'm going to get us something to drink."

"I don't want anything. Help yourself. You know where it is."

He went to the kitchen, came back with a glass, which he set on the mantel. She was still standing in front of the fire. He said, "I love you."

"Josh, don't."

"I do." He started to put his arms around her.

She stepped back. "I don't want to be touched right now. Drink your drink. I've told you these things because I like you, I trust you as much as—maybe more than—anybody I've ever known. It's only fair that you should know why I'm not . . . why I can't . . ."

"Bull." He said it calmly, reached for his glass, surveying her over the edge of it. "You've had some psych courses yourself, honey, read some books, and ended up with a screwed-up, mud-pie image of yourself that you've patted into shape and set on a shelf to dry. A 'poor little Gigi' doll, from which you sometimes derive a bit of pleasure."

"I've got a swell idea—go home. All right?"

"No." He swirled his drink, ice cubes tinkling. "Of course, if you've got a masochistic thing that needs not to be loved, if this is how you get your kicks—"

"Please shut up!" Her eyes flashed a pale-blue fire. "I hate the psychological jargon that people use as a substitute for real thinking. There are certain slots that they'd fold all of us into—stuffing, bending to fit. Oh, I am beginning to be very sorry I ever let you find out so much about me!"

"I am very glad you did. It gives you a dimension that helps me understand why you are as you are. There have been times when I've thought Gigi Lang must be a pretty cold fish. I've been on the verge of breaking things off—not that there's ever been much to break off."

Anger faded from her eyes, leaving them full of misery. "I'm glad you didn't, although I know you should for your own good. I know I'm messed up. I've always known that, and always wanted terribly to be like everybody else. Sometimes I made an awful fool of myself trying. I was a weird little kid, Josh. I laughed a lot, louder than anybody else, to try to keep the kids from knowing I wasn't okay, like them. I pretended I wasn't afraid of anything. One time our fifth grade went to the Children's Museum. At the 'petting farm' they had a snake. I was the only girl in our class who would pick it up. There I was, laughing, holding that snake. I nearly blacked out."

He said, "Darling."

"I told a lot of lies. Things about my mother and what all we used to do before she died of"—she gave him a flat smile—"heart trouble."

"Heart trouble?"

"Yeah. I had been told by my grandfather, when I got old enough to ask, that my mother died because she got very tired and her heart just stopped. So I used to go around feeling of my heart, thinking it was about to stop. I would lie in bed at night and listen to it, knowing that if it didn't thump the next time, I would die. I was afraid to get tired, to run and do things. I even told the kids I had heart trouble."

"How old were you when you found out the truth about your mother?"

"I was nine, maybe ten. One of the kids on our street told me. So now I went from one hang-up to another. I knew that I hadn't inherited a heart that was about to stop, but I knew my mother had died because she wanted to. She hadn't loved me enough to want to stay with me. Of her own free will, she had just left me."

"And that was worse."

"Much. Because it destroyed all the fantasies I'd had about her. Oh, I went on to some others—lies—about my glamorous grandmother in Spain, the one who sent me all the presents—pearls, a sapphire ring, stuff no kid needs—and I told about how she was begging me to come live with her, but my grandfather couldn't bear to part with me, and blah, blah, blah. And then this same mean, rotten little kid, Elsie Semelweiss, told me that my grandmother was a whore. We had this awful fight—we scratched and hit and pulled hair—and I ran home bawling and hid in the closet under the stairs. My grandfather found me there when he came home and put away his hat, my dress all torn, still bawling."

"Your grandfather wasn't the sort of person you would run to, but you hid where you knew he would find you."

"I guess so. Sure, I must have. So we went into his study and he shut the door so the housekeeper wouldn't hear. He sat at his desk and I sat in a chair. Grandfather didn't have lips—just a line under his gray mustache where his mouth was. And he told me in his proud, bitter way that my grandmother was an immoral woman. So, at twelve, I was already disillusioned, not expecting anything from anybody. Not even myself. Ashamed that all the kids knew what a liar I was. He sent me to boarding school, where there were a lot of rich kids nobody wanted to have around, and . . ."

Gently, Josh said, "You cling, don't you, just a little—please try not to get angry, Gigi—to the idea that you had a rotten childhood?"

"I did have a rotten childhood."

"You did, but—"

"You can't possibly understand. You had a great child-hood, with a family that loved you. I grew up with a feeling of being abandoned, not worth loving. Maybe there is a bit of the masochist in me. I have recognized that, tried to fight against it, put it behind me and go on to other things. Not very wisely. The relationships with all those guys . . ."

"Were you just throwing yourself away because of this feeling that you weren't worth very much?"

"Maybe. But it didn't work, Josh."

"Because you do know that you are worth something."

"Yes. I'm not willing to give up on that yet."

"Neither am I."

"I even know that there are a few little things about myself to like. My honesty, for one. I don't lie to myself. Also, I can look at some of the other persons in my life with some kindness, now that I'm older. Some understanding. Now that Grandfather is gone, I can remember him with compassion, even some affection."

"That's good."

"He tried, within his limits. For instance, he gave me good presents. His kind of thing—I think he was hoping I'd grow up to be a scientist, you know, something worthwhile. One time he gave me a terrarium—"

"You mentioned that under hypnosis."

"Did I? Gosh, I loved that thing. I stuck little stones in it for stepping stones, and a piece of mirror for a lake. I would sit staring at it for the longest time, with all those tiny little things growing in it. And I would imagine myself, tiny, living there, with the plants like trees over my head. My own dear, safe, little world where nobody could see me." She cocked her head. "Am I scaring you? Are you wondering about my mental health?"

"No."

"And Mimi. I was terribly resentful of her for a while. I hated her. All those effusive, extravagant protests of how much she loved me, and how much she wished Grandfather would let her have me, but the schools, darling, on Majorca were really quite impossible, and anyhow, she had to be free to travel, precious, with what's-his-name."

Josh was smiling at the mimicking of her grandmother's voice.

"I can remember at boarding school reading those letters out loud to my friends and showing them her picture. They said she looked like a movie star. I was so ugly then. For years I had a pewter-gray smile because of the braces to keep my teeth back. I was awkward, self-conscious."

He put his hand on her hair, trailed his fingers down along her cheek. "Were you, Gigi?"

"Yes, truly. I was awful inside and out. Kids like us go into sort of a reverse snobbishness—we'd compete to see who could tell the worst things. I won. Nobody else had a grandmother who was a whore, so busy batting around Europe that she couldn't be bothered with an orphan child. It was true that she couldn't be bothered, but I can see now that it really was no setup for a child."

"And she didn't come back at all to this country?"

"Not until my grandfather died. I was in college."

"And how did you feel about her when you finally got to know her?"

"I was crazy about her. She was clever, fun, funny. She's been back nearly every summer since then. She can walk down the street and make friends with everybody—children, old men, dogs, everybody. She wants everybody to be happy, wants everybody to love her because she loves everybody. But—and this wasn't a letdown, because I had already sensed it—Mimi loves, has always loved, herself best of all."

He mused, "Nothing you've said yet has sold her to me. The aging jet setter is not my favorite type. Come to think of it, I don't believe I've ever known one."

"Josh Lincoln, you would adore her. She would force you to adore her. I know exactly what she is, see right through her, but I accept her. And I wouldn't trade her for anybody's conventional grandmother. Heavens, no, not my Mimi."

"But after your grandfather died, there was no reason why you couldn't have gone there."

"That's what I thought. I'd have quit college in a minute. But in her charming, almost believable way, she kept telling me that she *longed* to have me come, but that it was a shame not to finish my education in this country. Summers? Well, they were *beastly* hot on Majorca, so she never stayed there. But next summer—it was always next summer —maybe Switzerland? And the next, maybe Ireland? I got my passport once, but there was some awfully good reason, I forget what now, why she couldn't have me come. I think the truth may have been—part of the truth—that a grown-up grandaughter would have dated her. Maybe she had to keep up the pretense of youth to keep this guy."

"Have you ever met him?"

"No. He always goes to England—that's his home— when she comes here. He has a hyphenated name— Trevelyan-Jones. Don't you love it? Richard Trevelyan-Jones."

"A fortune hunter?"

"I shouldn't think so. He has something to do with films on the Continent. Very talented, Mimi says. I'll meet him, I suppose, when I go. Then I'll know more about him."

"You really are going?"

"This May, I think. That's a very good month there, she says. And this time"—she held up crossed fingers—"this time I think she really does want me to come. Wait a minute. I'll get you her last letter and read you a couple of things she says."

Gigi went into the bedroom and came back with a letter and some pictures. She handed him first a studio portrait in a silver frame. It showed a mischievous, elfin face, elegantly boned, somewhat dated by the bouffant hairstyle, but it was the face of a young woman.

Josh read the slashing scrawl: "All the love in the world, Mimi."

"She must have been around fifty when she sent me that. Can you believe it?"

"No."

"I was in boarding school and I kept it in a drawer." She sorted through some color snapshots. "Look at this one. I'm not sure of her age, but she's got to be in her sixties now." She handed him a picture of a lithe figure on a surfboard. The hair was shoulder-length, a flyaway, shining flame. The white bikini she wore set off the lightly tanned skin and youthful body. Her head was thrown back, laughing.

He frowned in perplexity. "Good heavens, when was this taken?" He reached for the other snapshots.

"I took that when she was here last June. That's exactly how she is, always laughing. Laughter is the best medicine, she always says. Of course, she'd had her face lifted twice that I know of, and maybe everything else too. They do that now, you know. You aren't listening."

"Yes, I am. I was just thinking. I've got a grandmother too—had, that is. She was a devout pessimist all her life. She used to say to me and my brothers, 'Laugh in the morning, cry before night.' It would have made a great bumper sticker if she hadn't been too scared to drive. Go ahead, you were going to read me some of her letter."

The girl unfolded the letter, many-paged, flamboyantly written with a pen whose spreadable point gave emphasis to the many exclamation points and much underlining.

"This was the last letter I had from her, written in October. She doesn't write often, but when she does, she gets carried away." She started leafing through the pages, smiling from time to time. "When I read her letters, I can just hear her voice. This isn't the part I wanted to read you, but listen . . .

"'Tell me about yourself, darling child, you never do. Are you living with some nice boy? Or are you living with several? Is it true what I hear about group sex in the States these days? *Mon Dieu*, I feel myself on the verge of a lecture—it turns out I'm a bit *stodgy*, after all, and I've considered myself so *worldly* all these years!!! But I do *mourn* the days when sex was naughty and fun and not a group exercise recommended for one's psychological health. The secrecy, the intrigues were so *delicious*!!!'"

Josh was grinning. "She seemed never to have been very secretive."

"Consistency is not one of Mimi's jewels. Here's the part I was looking for: 'I *long* to see you. This time I will not take no for an answer!!!' As if I ever said no. 'Try for April or May. Yes, May. It's perfect then. I do hope you'll have been on your job long enough to have those yummy travel benefits you airline people get. I plan a quiet winter. My sweet, but somewhat tiresome, doctor has suggested that I should rest—*me*!!! But I'll admit that I'm not too undone at having an excuse for breakfast in bed and so on. Rest does do such marvels for one's looks—you know how *vain* I am!!! So I'll save my strength and be ready for a real wing-ding when you come. We'll tear up the island! I know some of the *most* divine people. We are simply a-swarm with counts and barons and titles of all kinds, also rich Americans who can sometimes be bearable too. Precious, dearest child, you are my own, my only, flesh and blood, and I long, long, *long* to see you! I have moments of being forced to admit (though only to myself and to you, *chérie*) that I am not getting any younger. But, do you know, I am actually *much* younger than Dietrich? I've told some shocking lies about my age, but that's the *truth*! And my legs aren't bad either!!!"

Josh was nodding, laughing a little. "She sounds like fun. I'd like to meet the old girl. I can see why you feel as you do about her. Now, let me make a suggestion."

"Okay, since you're my guru."

"Before you think about seeing a hypnoanalyst—"

"I'm not thinking about it. You are."

"All right. I am. But don't you think that first it might be sensible to ask Mimi if she can throw any light on this thing that seems to worry you so much? She may be able to give you a simple, logical explanation that will relieve your mind."

"Like what? Josh, I've tried and tried to think."

"Beats me. But what harm could there be in writing to her and telling her just what has happened both times when you've been regressed?"

5

By the time Josh left, it was very late. Not sleepy, Gigi sat at the desk in her bedroom, pulled out writing paper, and started the letter.

"Darling Mimi . . ."

How could she say it? Darling Mimi, a non-stop talker, always preferred to stick to safe subjects. She talked of films, the theater, hair styles, clothes—she had been perplexed by the hippie look. She always had amusing tidbits of international gossip concerning her celebrity friends. If she had any creed at all, it must be, "Laugh and the world laughs with you." Gigi knew that her grandmother might very well give her questions an airy brush-off—if she bothered to reply to them at all.

For a few minutes she nibbled at the end of her pen. "You are a dear to say you want me to come to Majorca, and I am planning to come in May. But Josh Lincoln (no, I am not living with him, but he's my boss at World Wide, and I see him a lot and trust his good judgment) has suggested that I write to you and ask you some questions about something that is worrying me a bit . . . Okay, quite a lot, or I wouldn't be writing you this letter . . ."

She stopped again to think, then plunged in. "I know you are unhappy when I try to talk to you about my mother. I understand why you have always been reluctant to talk about her, particularly about her death. As you know, I was too young to remember anything at all. It has always seemed rather a blessing that I couldn't remember. But something seems to have stuck there in the craw of my subconscious. (Now, don't stop reading yet, this is very important.) Twice, under hypnosis, I have been regressed to that bad Christmas week when she died. Each time I have become very excited—so I am told—almost as if I were there again, seeing. And I screamed these words: 'Witch, witch! Mommy, Mommy! No, no!'

"There is a good chance that this will turn out to be something trivial, of no importance. In fact, that is what I am hoping you may be able to tell me. Maybe—hey, this just hit me!—there was some kind of fiesta that week, with people in costumes who might have been frightening to a little American girl. I wish you would think back, try hard, and see if you can remember anything whatsoever about my having been taken to a parade or something of the sort, and let me hear from you right away."

She went back and underlined the last words, knowing the long stretches between Mimi's letters. "I have had a few problems. I've never bothered you with them. I saw the school psychiatrist—a real jerk—a few times, but I am convinced that the best psychoanalysis is self-analysis. I know you've never been one to fool around with those people! My feeling is that if I can just understand *why* I am as I am, then I'll be able to get on with the business of *who* I am. Very likely—and this also just occurred to me, since what I am doing is thinking on paper—the thing is that I really want to be a little bit more like you, and just have fun and shake off my guilt feelings, and take it from there.

"Josh, who is trying to help me get my head together, can, I'm pretty sure, be conned into hypnotizing me again, although he insists that he is not in the business and tells me that I should see a real hypnoanalyst.

"What I want to get back to—and this is the crux of the matter—is the feeling of my mother's love for me. I have a thing about it. It may not make much sense to you, but I've got to get my head straightened out, and this may be the way I can do it. After all, some people spend fifty bucks an hour trying to unscramble their kinked-up brains, and I think my own little handy-dandy do-it-yourself scheme is worth a try. Only, I need help from somebody who was there. Who else but you, Mimi?"

She read back over what she had written, trying to imagine her grandmother's reaction when she read it. For a few minutes she considered tearing the whole thing up and starting the letter all over again, but she wasn't sure she could come any closer to saying what she wanted to say.

"You now owe me two letters—no, three, counting this one. I did send you a flabbergasted note of thanks for your Christmas gift, but come to think of it, you have never let me know if you got what I sent you. Never mind, it was nothing compared to that fabulous diamond ring. It's a bit too small—your hands are dainty compared to mine, and anyhow I'm afraid to wear it until it's insured. I'll take care of that right away, and then the customers and my buddies at World Wide will wonder why I work at all if I'm that rich." Mimi didn't have to know that the ring didn't fit at all into her image of herself.

"Write me the day you get this—*el mismo día*. My Spanish is not very good, but I think that's close enough. Like instantly. Don't fail me."

Gigi signed the letter With Love, sealed it, stamped it, and then propped it up on the desk so she wouldn't forget to mail it tomorrow.

It was past one. She looked out the window. The snow had stopped falling and the moon shone on a fairyland of drifted white. She was glad the next day was Sunday; her driveway would take some shoveling before she could get her car out.

In the bathroom, taking off her make-up, she thought about Josh Lincoln. She felt pretty good about him now, almost a little bit good about herself. It had been a relief to tell him all those things she had never told anybody.

Remembering what he had said about her face, she smiled a little. *Some saint.* She thought about Steve and Mark and Buck and some of the others she had known during the bad year when she had tried to throw herself away. Their names were strung together like a barbed-wire rosary. It would be a relief if she didn't feel she had to finger those abrasive names any more. Josh knew now, and still said he loved her. She supposed she would go with him someday to Ohio to meet his family, his farmer father and his prize-winning, dahlia-growing mother. She was not even very sure what a dahlia looked like, but she supposed she could pretend that she cared.

In bed, she turned off the light. The room was still full of a brilliant light that, coming through the Venetian blinds, made a ladder that looked as if it would be strong enough for angels to descend on. She lay there, awed by the strangeness of it, awed by the equally strange knowledge that she felt a little bit comforted about herself after all those words tonight.

When she slept, she dreamed that someone was caressing her toes. Someone said, "Poor baby." Not Catalina. Josh. She moved to make room for him on the bed, gave herself to his urgent embrace, as, awake, she had never been able to do.

She woke too soon. The bright light in the room was only a temporary light of moon on snow that would melt with the reality of days to come. The urgent need in her dream was that same old need that had been met—and met—and met—by those with the barbed-wire names. It was not their fault that nothing had ever lasted.

"What is the matter with you, Gigi?" they had said, puzzled, nice enough guys. "What is the *matter* with you?"

As Josh Lincoln someday might say, adding another link to that barbed-wire chain.

The moonlight showed her the white square of her letter propped up over there by her purse. She thought about Mimi. She would be very much surprised if she ever received a satisfactory answer to it.

She could visualize the splayed lines of Mimi's writing now: "Cry and you cry alone . . ."

6

IN ski pants and boots, Gigi tramped through the snow
to the little shopping center to mail Mimi's letter in
time for the one Sunday pickup. She shoveled a path then
to her front door, moved snow from in back of her car so
that she could get out in the morning, put hot water in
the bird bath to melt the snow and ice, filled the bird feeder,
and then, after watching the pampered cardinals for a while,
left the heady outdoor wonderland and went inside with
reluctance to do the necessary chores, such as laundry, to
get ready for the week ahead. After she had washed her
hair, she applied a mild bleach. It was packed now under
a plastic covering to complete the lightening process, and
she was sitting at the kitchen table manicuring her nails.

She held them out, smooth ovals under a coat of clear polish, admiring them, admiring herself for having stopped biting them. She used to gnaw them like a nervous beaver, right down to the quick. One tiny milestone, kicking that habit. It was a small thing to be proud of.

The phone rang. Josh said, "I feel like taking you to dinner."

Gigi sopped at a drip that threatened one eye. "I'm all ready."

"There is this place near Leesburg called The Smokehouse. You walk in past all these smoked country hams and slabs of bacon, past all the home-canned pickles and apple butter. You duck under strings of Indian corn and gourds and walk around kegs of molasses and cider . . ."

Night had fallen when they walked past all that. The interior was dimly lit and heavy with the smell of hickory smoke. They sat first in a small parlor for hot mulled cider, which they stirred with sticks of cinnamon. Because of the gasoline shortage, crucial just then, they had the place almost to themselves.

Gigi had dressed up a little in pale-blue sweater and matching slacks. "I like it. I love it," she said, her gaze taking in the braided rugs on the random-width pine floors, the framed prints and maps and documents on the walls. "I keep looking for something that's fake, but it all looks real."

"Why can't you just accept things without question for what they seem to be?"

"I don't know. It's wrong, isn't it? Because if I keep looking, I'll find something I'd rather not know about. Like, maybe the beams aren't real, or the worm holes. Like, those handwritten labels on those jars out there are maybe just pasted on over labels that say Heinz 57 Varieties. Like, maybe the floors are just that clever linoleum."

"They're real. I can see splinters."

"Good. I like splinters."

He was leaning back, looking at her in that way of his as if he saw right through her. He wore a black turtleneck sweater under a rather worn tweed sports coat. Gigi said, "You look real. Don't ever get that tooth capped, the one that's a little bit crooked."

"I'll cancel my appointment first thing in the morning."

"I'm not entirely real, you know. My hair isn't this light and my eyelashes aren't this dark. One thing, though, I don't wear a padded bra."

A smile quirked. "I know."

"Mimi tried once to get me to have those silicone things implanted. She said she'd pay for them. Fifteen hundred dollars. Imagine. They attach them with little Dacron patches to your chest wall, gulp. And then everything grows over and nobody can tell."

"You would tell. You with your compulsive honesty."

She gave her funny little infectious laugh.

Josh said, "May I talk for a while now? I mean, if you're through baring your chest and telling me all these fascinating things I didn't ask about. Last night you told me an awful lot of things that I would never have asked about."

"I thought you should know. I mean, before a guy decides he loves a girl . . ."

"You don't *decide* about love, Gee. You decide to buy a car, or change jobs, or take karate lessons, but love isn't a decision. It either hits you or it doesn't."

"It has never hit me. I've just gone ahead without being hit—you know, hoping. I'll never do that again."

"I hope you won't."

The waitress came to take their order for dinner, a country girl with red cheeks and chapped hands. The menu was written on a slate with chalk. They decided on broiled mountain trout, but Josh asked the girl to hold it for a while and bring them some more mulled cider.

Gigi watched the girl as she walked away. "Was that touch just a little bit fakey—the slates—trying just a little too hard for ye old-timey touch?"

"Oh, shut *up*, sweetie. Relax, enjoy, listen to what I'm going to say. As usual, you got me off the track. I want to talk about Christmas. I can't wait."

"We just had it—remember? You went home."

"Right. I asked you to go with me and you said no. Did you have a tree?"

"For one? Oh, Josh, Christmas doesn't mean anything to me. It's just a plastic, canned-music season to get through, and—"

"Never mind. Last night under hypnosis you told about a Christmas when you were eight, I think you said. You went to the club."

"We always did."

"Next Christmas you're going home with me."

Gigi sipped her cider. She said warily, "I have the feeling that your family is the kind who thinks when their son brings a girl home for Christmas, it means something."

"Yes, that's what they think. I'll let you be the one to tell them we're just good friends. We'll get there about supper-time. Oyster stew, that's traditional at our house, every Christmas Eve, because of the big feed that's coming the next day. Right after supper, the tree is dragged in. Dad and the twins have cut it in the woods."

"It sounds very Currier-and-Ivesy."

"It is. Try not to sound sophisticated. The ornaments come down from the attic, the same ornaments that I can remember from all the years of my life. First, on top, goes the silver star that I cut out when I was in the first grade. A disgrace to the whole tree, that bent twenty-year-old star, but my mother says she always remembers how I looked when I brought it home to her—no front teeth. Mothers are queer for—don't ask me why—little kids with no front teeth. And then there are some paper chains the boys made and the ornaments that came from Germany which my mother bought when she was studying music, before she got married, when, I guess, she thought she was going to be a concert pianist. And there are some little carved wooden things from Sweden—my father's mother was Swedish. And there are a thousand balls—my mother always buys new ones because the dogs have broken some of them—and popcorn balls and candy canes and strings of cranberries. By now the tree is a mess. You can hardly see it. But then the lights are turned on and everybody always says it's the prettiest tree we ever had. By then it's late. We go to the midnight service. We walk, that's how close it is."

Gigi said faintly, "Josh Lincoln, I never even went to Sunday School. I don't think I'd fit in."

"Hush. All you'd have to do is sit there, maybe sing carols a little—you wouldn't have to know the words. It's pretty nice. My mother plays the organ. There are candles and poinsettias and a forest of woodsy-smelling greens. They always have a program. When the twins were about five, Mike was a shepherd and John was a wise man. And Mike slugged John because he kept stepping on his bathrobe. Last year one of the cherubs in the Bethlehem choir picked her nose all the way through 'Away in a Manger.'"

Gigi gave him a bit of a smile. "Could I go just as a friend?"

"I don't plan for our 'friendship' to last for eleven months. We'll go home then, crunching through snow if it's like most Christmases. You and I will have the guest room. There's a quilt on the big double bed that my great-great-grandmother made."

"You are saying that your parents think it's okay for friends to sleep together?"

"You know what I'm saying, Gee. Try not to interrupt. The next morning is relatively calm for a while. The presents are opened, then the dogs go mad in a sea of wrapping paper. Dinner at one. Big, traditional. The table groans. We groan. My mother says that next year she's not going to have so many vegetables and desserts. My father says that's how he likes it. Every year, the same dialogue. That afternoon, except for the twins, who are out riding whatever they got for Christmas, everybody takes a nap. We'll take a nap."

Gigi didn't interrupt, just looked at him. *No fair, Josh Lincoln, you know I've never slept under anybody's great-great-grandmother's quilt.*

"That night, the big party. All the people on the farm come with their families. The kids run wild and the babies bawl. All the relatives come. Aunt Nita, she's the rich one, sort of amused by it all. Aunt Nita has Taste. Her tree is decorated with white doves, she told us last year, just white doves. Aunt Alma comes with Alma-Jean. She's fifteen, same age as the twins, and a musical prodigy. They hate Alma-Jean—naturally; she was picking out tunes on the piano about the time they were learning to wave bye-bye. She always plays. Brilliantly. Her mother always passes around rave notices from the newspapers to prove it. But Alma-Jean does funny things with her elbows and she sways and her glasses slide down on her nose. The twins get hysterical. My mother sends them to their room, where last year they played acid rock. Everybody goes home. Finally.

The house is a mess, with popcorn balls crunched into the rugs and cranberry jelly smeared. Last year some kid threw up in the aspidistra."

"The what?"

"Aspidistra. That's a plant my mother has. She said never again. Every year she says that." He stopped. Gigi was looking down at her nails. "Okay if I tell you some more?"

"Sure. I'm listening." She folded her nails into her palms and resisted the urge to start biting.

"We go skating on the lake when the ice is thick enough. In the boathouse there is a record player with a loud-speaker. My parents skate, hands crossed. They're still in love. When there's snow we coast down the hills on this big toboggan that holds ten people. We get out the sleigh and go jingling up hill and down dale—and if the whole thing sounds corny, that's only because it is. But it's real, it's true, and I love it. I'll go back there to live someday, I suppose, if the girl I marry would like to. The farm is a fairly big operation. My father has been saying he could use a business manager."

They ate on a red-checked tablecloth under a low-timbered ceiling. The glow of candles in red-glass holders gave a dim, flickering light. Gigi was very quiet, not doing justice to the broiled trout.

"You're not eating."

"It's awfully good. I'm not very hungry." She pushed the food around on her plate.

"I wish you'd say something."

"I've been thinking, Josh. What if I wanted white doves on my Christmas tree?"

"You could have them."

"I don't even want white doves. But what I am saying is that I don't want to have to fit myself into anybody else's way of life. I don't want to let myself in for a life of pretending to be something I'm not. I'm afraid that if I ever went there, I would be so crazy about them that I would . . ."

"They would be crazy about you, Gee."

Gigi pushed her plate away and steadied her chin on tight-folded hands. She said, her lips barely moving, "Would they be glad you love a girl who has broken every rule?" She tried to smile.

A long pause. Too long. He said, "They brought me up to make my own choices."

"Why don't you answer my question?"

"I did. That's all the answer that's necessary. They would love the girl I have chosen to love. Do you want dessert?"

"No. Just coffee. They would ask more than I have to give."

"Everything. For me, they want everything. So do I. But I'm not asking more than you have to give."

She said rapidly, "You want a girl just like the girl who married dear old what's-his-name. A girl who would give up her career as a concert pianist."

"Do you play?"

She refused to return his smile. "You know what I mean."

"I don't think my mother gave up anything she didn't want to give up. Ask her about that when you see her."

She was shaking her head. "I'm not sure I'll ever see her."

They said little more. At her door, Gigi said she didn't want him to come in. He kissed her goodnight. It began that way. It got to be a kiss that could have lasted the night.

She turned her head. "I won't add your name to that list. I won't—I won't." Her voice sounded close to tears.

Josh stepped back. "I don't want my name on that list. I want a new page. The first page of a whole new book."

When he had gone and she was taking down the clothes she had washed earlier, she remembered what Josh had said about love: it just hits you. She was not sure he was right, but she wished it would hit her. Total commitment. That was what Josh wanted.

She folded pantyhose and put them neatly in a drawer. She selected a white blouse to wear in the morning, hung it with her airline uniform. If she had written a diary of all the minutes of her life, there would be no word about love. Affection, friendship, passion. But they were peripheral emotions surrounding a void.

She felt hollow with the need for it to be filled, sad with the knowledge that it might remain empty. But she had too much respect for Josh Lincoln to pretend she had the capacity for love for him or anybody else.

7

The weekend had been an emotional binge. With relief, Gigi slid into the familiar work pattern the next morning. She stood behind the airline counter, smiling, answering questions, writing tickets, thanking, laughing. Her pale hair was brushed back from her face neatly. Her pearl-gray uniform was spotless, with crisp white collar and cuffs showing. Silver hoops were in her ears this morning. Her eyes, shadowed with luminous gray, were silver, barely blue. No one could have guessed that she had slept very little the night before.

She said to a sleepy-looking customer, "Omaha? World Wide doesn't have a direct flight, sir. Sorry. You'll have a two-hour wait in Chicago at O'Hare . . . Yes, the flight's wide open, plenty of seats." She reached for a ticket.

Josh stood at her elbow. He said low, pretending to look over the flight schedule, "I had a hell of a night."

"Oh, what a shame, sir."

"You know what the whole trouble is?"

"I am sure you can tell me." She started writing the ticket for Omaha.

"That damned book you read. A guy has a theory about emotional death and you slide right into it."

"Because it fits." She looked across the counter. "Seat preference, sir?" The man was smoking, looking off into the distance. He didn't hear her. She put him down for the smoking section.

Josh said, "And you're perfectly happy."

"I'm not perfectly happy."

"Perfectly happy to be perfectly miserable."

"I'm not perfectly miserable." Gigi reached for the credit card the man had laid on the counter. "You should have been a psychiatrist, boss. The one I went to was always trying to get me to say his words about myself."

"Did he ever say I love you, I want to marry you, hang-ups and all?"

"Nope. He had too much sense for that." She was about to slide the ticket across the counter when Josh reached for it. "What are you doing, dum-dum? You forgot to imprint the ticket with the credit card."

Gigi gave an apologetic smile to the customer, stamped her foot for Josh's benefit, and ran the ticket through the machine. "You've got me so rattled I don't know what I'm doing. We've got about two hundred people going out in the next half-hour. Haven't you got anything better to do—like back in your office? If I were the boss of this outfit, I'd fire you. Bothering the female employees." She pushed the ticket and the credit card across the counter, thanked the

Omaha-bound passenger, gave him a smile that was automatically dazzling, then turned her attention to the next in line.

"Am I?" Josh stood so close that his thigh was against hers. "Bothering you, that is?"

"Yes!" She said it out of the side of her mouth, busying herself with the next ticket.

"Good."

"Who's going to do the will-call tickets for tomorrow?"

"You. I sent Carol to help that woman in the wheelchair."

Her head down, writing, she said, "Why don't you at least pretend to be doing something useful? That girl at the end of the counter, the new one, Miss D-cup, we call her, is watching us."

"I am watching her, actually. That's why I'm out here. Thought it was you, didn't you? She messed up her deposit yesterday. You were the one who broke her in, I happen to know."

"You were the one who hired her, I happen to know."

"You better believe I hired her. Her daddy is one of the top dogs in Chicago. He's my boss's boss. Do you want me to end up back on the farm before I'm ready?"

"Why don't you send her to empty ashtrays in the VIP room? That takes no brains."

"What she likes to do is pour drinks in there. Or ride the mobile lounge when celebrities are aboard. Arthur Godfrey was here yesterday—he knows her father—and she took a coffee break that lasted until noon and then had lunch with him. P.R. is important, I know, but . . ."

An elderly man leaned across the counter to inquire anxiously, "Where is the ladies' room?"

"The ladies' . . . ?"

"Yes. I'm supposed to meet my wife outside."

"Oh. Just around the corner on your left, sir, can't miss it. Not at all, sir."

Lines were growing longer in front of the World Wide counter and at Pan Am and United. Josh took over Carol's window next to Gigi. Feet in increasing numbers tapped, clumped, slapped, hurried, sauntered. The faces were blasé, tense, eager, blank. Arrivals were announced, departures. A Miss Zenia Brown was asked to pick up the courtesy phone. The day was under way.

Gigi smiled at a man who chewed gum nervously. "Smoking or non-smoking."

"Non. I'm trying to quit."

She wrote, stamped, stapled, inserted, and handed over the long envelope. "Boarding time in about half an hour . . . Yes, it's on time . . . Thank *you*. Have a nice flight."
"Hi. Round trip to San Francisco? . . . Right, it's a lovely city. You'll confirm, won't you, twenty-four hours before coming back?"

She gave a bulkhead seat to a lady with a baby, bumping an irate VIP to do it. This job had its compensations.

Carol came hurrying in, the little swinging gate clicking behind her. She paused behind Gigi, who was busy with a customer, and said in her ear, "Wait till you hear what I just heard. You know that red-headed stewardess—TWA —and the pilot she always shacks up with when they're on layover here? Well . . ."

"Smoking or non-smoking? Okay, smoking . . . You may be right. Nobody lives forever and all that. When you gotta go, you gotta go." Her laugh. "Your baggage checks are stapled." She turned. "What, Carol?"

Carol, who had replaced Josh at the next window, began writing, stamping, stapling, inserting busily as she said to

Gigi, ". . . and there she sat on the bed. His *wife*. I mean, when they walked into the motel room. She's not even going to give him visiting privileges."

"Wow."   "A personal check, sir? . . . Yes, we do. May I see two forms of identification, please? . . . American Express and a driver's license will be fine." His driver's license had his picture on it. She glanced up. Same beak on both. "Yes, that's fine. I don't need anything more . . . Not at all. Happy to. Have a nice flight."

A girl with a sleeping bag and carry-on luggage.

"One way to Madrid via London? . . . Yes, Heathrow, no problem."

"I've saved up for a year."

"Have you really? Good for you. Know any Spanish— *habla usted español*?"

"Not much. *Poco, muy poco*. But I've got a phrase book. They tell me I can get by."

Gigi picked up the pile of bills, made change. "I hope they're right. That's what I'll have to depend on mostly. I'm going to Spain myself in May—Majorca, that is. Seems a long time off. Can't wait . . ."

Just six days later, a working Sunday, Gigi returned from lunch to find a number scrawled on her memo pad, together with *Urgent* written beneath it. She dialed the number, gave her name.

"Yes," said a voice, "one moment, please." And then, "I have a cablegram for you from Palma de Majorca."

Majorca? "Read it, please."

"It says, 'Very ill. Come at once. I need you.' It is signed, 'Mimi.'"

"Thank you." Gigi put back the phone.

The passenger agent who was working at Carol's window

gave her a concerned look. "What is it? You look kind of shook up, Gee."

"A cablegram from Mimi, my grandmother. She's very ill. She wants me to come to Majorca at once."

"What are you going to do?"

"Go, of course, right away. Please fix me up for the next flight to Palma."

Josh was in his office. He got up from his desk when she told him and came to put an arm across her shoulders. "Sure, you can get off. No problem here. You have to go, but I'm not sure I think you ought to break your neck to get there. Your grandmother may not be all that ill."

"I'm afraid she is." Gigi repeated the exact words of the message.

"Sit down for a minute."

Gigi sat on the edge of a chair and looked at him, her eyes wide and bleak. "It's what she said about needing me. I never had the feeling that she ever really needed me before. But now I think that she does. Blood ties—you know, all that. She admitted that she wasn't in tiptop shape in her letter—remember? Oh, Josh, I wish you could have met her when she was . . ."

"Oh, I expect to. She'll pull out of this and be fine again if she's the gutsy girl you say she is."

"I don't mean to sound as if I think she won't make it, or anything like that. I'm sure they have perfectly good doctors in Majorca, and she's always been so healthy."

"She probably received your letter. Or did it have time to get there?"

"Oh, yes, I think so."

"Well, there you are. She got your letter and it made her homesick to see you."

"Maybe you're right. I don't think I said anything to

upset her. I did ask some questions that you told me to ask, but I can't think there is any connection."

"You will know soon enough, so don't worry. You said you were going to try to make that plane tonight. Just tell me now what I can do to help."

"Nothing. I think I've got plenty of cash. And a couple of credit cards. I hope I can find my passport. I'm going to rush home now, pack, drive back here—"

"No. I'll come and get you. Then there won't be any problem about leaving your car."

She had located her passport, thrown some clothes into a bag—Majorca weather would surely be warmer than Washington—and was all ready and waiting when Josh got there. On the way out the door she stopped, her eyes round. "My ring—didn't I tell you about it? The big diamond she sent me for Christmas."

"Wear it. She'll expect you to."

"I can't get it on. My fingers are bigger than hers. I had thought I'd have it made larger so I could wear it when I went in May."

"Well, you shouldn't just leave it here."

"Shouldn't I? Maybe not. I'll get it if I can remember where I put it."

He followed her back into the bedroom. She poked through a couple of drawers, found a box of tangled costume jewelry, and held the ring toward him.

He looked at the stone with awe. "What a rock! It must be three carats, at least. Have you any idea what a diamond this size may be worth?"

"Nope. A lot, I suppose. I really hate diamonds, and can't imagine ever wearing that thing where anybody I know would see it. It's a sin, with people hungry."

"There are people who wouldn't have to be hungry to bop you over the head for a ring like that."

"Maybe. Anyhow, you keep it."

"I'll have it made larger. What size do you wear?"

"How would I know?"

"I might need to know—like someday when I buy you a friendship ring."

"I want silver. Doesn't have to be sterling." She poked some more in the box. "Here's my class ring. It's the right size."

He put both rings in his pocket. "Come on. We don't have that much time if you're going to be on that plane."

A privileged person because of his job, Josh walked back with her along the wide rows of seats on the big 747. "A light load tonight, for a wonder. You can ask for a blanket and pillow and stretch out. You'll be in London before you know it, and then in Majorca by midafternoon."

"Be sure to send that cable to say I'm coming and on what plane and everything. Don't lose that memo I wrote out for you. I want to be sure I'm met."

"So do I. So you send me a cable and tell me. Fasten your seat belt." He was sitting beside her.

"Oh, Josh. Just because I've never been anywhere . . ."

"Well, you never have, and you're kind of a dum-dum sometimes. Not always." He ran his hand back through her hair. "My mother has promised me that if she ever develops a messy-headed yellow dahlia, she'll name it Gigi."

"I bleach my hair. The roots are dark."

"So? If she ever comes up with a messy-headed yellow dahlia with dark roots . . ."

She threw her arms around him, kissed him, clung, suddenly reluctant to leave him.

74

A stewardess who knew Josh leaned to touch his shoulder. "Unless you're planning to leave on this plane, big boy . . ."

Josh got up. He leaned for another quick kiss. "The cable, Gee. Don't forget."

Gigi watched him go along the aisle, saw him pause to exchange a few words with the cute stewardess. She looked at him the way all girls looked at Josh Lincoln.

What's the matter with me? she thought. I should feel jealousy. I should feel something. She waved one last time. The plane was moving. She leaned then to see the beautiful Dulles Airport. Eero Saarinen had designed it. It was said to be the most beautiful airport in the world, and she had never had a chance to see it before from this vantage point.

It fell away. The lights of Washington fell away. She put back her head and tried to think about Mimi. She adored Mimi.

But she did not, perhaps, love even her.

8

Tired enough to cry, Gigi sat in the Son San Juan Airport in Palma, looking toward the front doors, not knowing what to do. Nobody had met her. Should she hire a taxi to take her all those miles to Ca'n Cornitx?

Some sort of malfunction with the landing gears had held up the plane in London for hours. She had tried to telephone Ca'n Cornitx, but the operator had said something in rapid Spanish that sounded as if it could mean the line was out of order.

She looked at the few others who sat or wandered uncertainly, all with tired, rather blank faces and the look of being bound for nowhere. It was hard to believe what she had once heard, that this airport sometimes had more arrivals and departures in one day than the John F. Kennedy in New York.

Her mind had exhausted the possibilities of what could have happened. Someone had met her plane and then gone away, tired of waiting. A message had been left—she had inquired—but the person who took it had gone home, not bothering to inform the replacement on the next shift. Mimi was in the hospital and the cable—had Josh sent it?—had never reached anybody who could do anything about it.

Or—and this wouldn't surprise her one iota—Mimi herself would come rushing through the door, her hair on fire, giving little ecstatic screams, laughing off her illness and letting loose a few elegant curse words in a polyglot of language about that sweet, old fuddy-dud of a doctor who didn't know his ass from his elbow. Or perhaps she would blame the maddening Majorcan inability—part of their charm, darling—to do anything whatever on time.

A tall man with graying hair was coming toward her. He limped a little and carried a cane. He was looking at her steadily, smiling as he advanced.

"Gigi. You've got to be Gigi!"

"Richard . . . ?" She stood.

"Can this be the little girl I used to carry on my shoulders? You don't remember me?"

"No, but . . ." She saw now that in spite of receding hair, he looked like the man in a snapshot Mimi had once shown her. But that had not prepared her for the warmth of his smile, the quick enfolding of his arms.

He kissed her on both cheeks. "A Spanish kiss for you, my dear. Welcome to Majorca!" It was the first time she had ever heard anyone pronounce the "j" in Majorca. "Frightfully sorry to be so late, but the chap delivered your cable only about two hours ago. It must have arrived during siesta time—they refuse to bestir themselves, you know. Had to drive my fool head off. I was afraid you'd have given up and gone back to America!"

His accent was mildly British. Already she liked him much more than she had expected to. His easy friendliness gave the lie to the American notion that the British were cold. "I tried to telephone."

"Our phone's been out since mid-December—bloody nuisance."

"How is Mimi?"

"Not awfully fit, I'm afraid. Is this your only bag, love? Then come along."

"Just a minute. I have to send a cablegram." She dashed away, wrote, "Arrived safely. Richard met me," paid, and went back to Richard. Accommodating her steps to his slower ones, they walked toward the front door.

"She's all right though, Mimi? I mean, going to be all right?"

"Well—no, not all right. We'll talk about that later. Plenty of time. It's a hell of a long drive to Ca'n Cornitx."

It was dark when they went outside. Gigi shivered in the chill wind. "I hadn't known it would be cold . . ."

"No. They keep you from knowing, the crafty travel agents. They blat about the sunshine. The poor *turistas* from Northern Europe—you'll see them—arrive bare-armed, white shoes, all ready to bask in what's been sold them as tropical sunshine. Here we are."

They got into his small car. He told her it was a Seat, Spanish cousin to the Fiat. "Easy on petrol, which is frightfully dear here, you know."

Gigi's first impression of Palma, as they drove toward it along the wide airport road, was that, from a distance, it looked like a little Miami with all the tall, modern hotels.

But then she saw the windmills, their huge vanes attached to ancient stone towers, peaked on top, quite unlike any she had ever seen before. And then she saw the spires and the Gothic honey-gold mass of the floodlighted cathedral.

"Our finest showpiece," Richard said. "Started in twelve hundred and something. It took them nearly four centuries to finish it." He pointed. "To our left, on top of the hill overlooking the bay, see the circular towers. That's Bellver Castle—means beautiful sight. It was built first as a royal palace. Then it was a fortress, and at one time a prison, but now it has been turned into a museum. The Lonja, the merchant's hall over there, is something else that visitors should see. It's a fine example of Gothic architecture. The columns inside branch at the top like palm trees." He gave her a glance. "Please stop me if I bore you. I'm afraid I sound awfully like a tour guide. But if you're interested I'll bring you back and we can go through as many of these places as you like."

"I am interested, very much. But everything will depend on Mimi's condition."

"So many times she has said that she wanted you to see it all, the whole island. They're on their way to ruining parts of it, of course. When Mimi and I first came here in nineteen fifty-one, it was unspoiled, a paradise. But nothing remains the same. Alas, nothing."

Gigi said hesitantly, "Is Mimi really seriously ill?"

"Yes. My dear girl, I'm sorry to hit you with this so bluntly, since it's obvious you are not prepared. How much did she tell you in her last letter?"

"Very little. She did say that her doctor had told her to rest up a bit. But that was in October. Then I got the cable. But I've been hoping . . ."

Richard's hand reached for hers. He patted it a couple of

times, then he said quietly, "Don't hope. There is no hope. She has a malignancy and it has spread."

Disbelief. Gigi was so tired from her almost sleepless night on the plane that she had to struggle for a moment to comprehend that such words of finality had been spoken about Mimi . . . *Mimi*! "Richard, I can't believe—why didn't she write me—does she know?"

"Who can tell? You know how she is—*très gaie! Muy felicidad*! All must always be *júbilo*!"

They were passing through the heart of Palma now, lined with palm trees and gay with lighted shops. Gigi was silent, trying to adjust to what Richard had told her. In an obvious attempt to cheer her a bit, he was pointing out landmarks, some of which had survived from the time of the Arab occupation. He mentioned dates, names of kings, calling her attention to identifying details of architecture of the various periods.

"How old is the city?" Not that she could bring herself to care much right now, but politeness seemed to demand some response. More dates, more names of churches, monuments, parks.

Lights shuddered on the bay. In spite of the lateness of the hour, crowds of people thronged the streets as if it were the height of the tourist season. Quaint carriages moved primly, horse-drawn. Richard explained that he wanted to make a little detour through the old quarter to show her some of the old seignorial mansions and palaces.

Gigi wanted only to hurry on to Ca'n Cornitx, but it was interesting to hear that he and Mimi knew some of the owners and had been entertained in the fine houses. Stately old doorways, some of them arched, many topped with coats of arms, had elaborate carvings of flowers, leaves, shells, cherubs. Occasional open grillwork gave glimpses of gardens blooming beyond the walls. Even at night it could be seen that the city was immaculate, with no litter anywhere.

Gigi said, "They must sweep these sidewalks every day."

"More than once, I'm sure. An artist friend, quite a tidy chap, actually, stood one day sharpening his pencil before sketching a doorway that had caught his fancy. A furious woman came charging out with her broom to sweep up the tiny shavings, calling him a name that I suppose it was fortunate the poor bloke couldn't understand."

Out of one of the dark side streets, a nun came zooming on a motorcycle, her habit flying behind her.

Richard laughed at Gigi's startled exclamation. "One of the common sights of the island. The Church still dominates, but not without a few concessions to modern ways. Mimi said once that she believes the thought of the motorcycle may have replaced some of the more pious lures for a girl to give her life to God."

They left the city behind, driving north on an excellent straight road. Gigi held out her watch to see its dial by the dashboard lights. "How long will it take us to get there?"

"I've done it sometimes in an hour. The road is fairly new, much better than in the old days. It has some savage turns, though, a little further along, as you shall see."

Gigi pressed her hands together in her lap, aware of the urge to bite her nails. *Mimi. No hope. What will I say to her?* Her grandfather had died without warning, just dropped between one moment and the next. Word had come to her at school. A shock, but easier than a deathbed confrontation would have been between two who had never had anything much to say to each other. She and Mimi had always rattled on constantly, laughing a lot. With Mimi, there was always so much to laugh about. And now . . .

It seemed like a dream to be hurtling through the night with a stranger. A kind stranger, though. That helped. He may very well have dreaded the responsibility of having her come, Gigi thought, having to break the news. She must try not to make things more difficult for him.

They met few cars and nobody passed them. Now the road began to twist, making hairpin turns. Richard drove with skill and as much speed as possible, but the speedometer showed that sometimes he slowed to a fifteen-kilometer crawl.

From time to time the headlights flashed on terraced hillsides with miles of stone walls holding groves of olive trees, their leaves pale in the moonlight. Occasionally Gigi could see the grotesqueries of individual trees. Now a grossly pregnant woman with many breasts, lifting tortured arms. Now Siamese twins, leaning away from each other, but inseparably joined for hundreds of years. Some of the phallic protuberances would bear awesome examination by day, and perhaps disappear altogether in sane light.

Richard said, "A few of the olive trees are said to be two thousand years old, which may be a bit of an exaggeration. It is true, however, that some of the viaducts that bring water down from the mountains were built that long ago by the Romans. After a while, on our right, you may be able to see Puig Mayor." He spelled it for her, pronounced it "Pooch." "It's our highest mountain. These last few days the top has been covered with snow."

Now and then, naming towns whose names she would never remember, he waved toward a huddle of lights, a large star ruby on his little finger catching the light from the dashboard. "You'll want to do all this by daylight, of course."

"If Mimi is . . ."

He didn't answer, but then he was shifting gears.

Gigi persisted. "There could be a remission. Lots of times they have remissions that last for years."

Richard was shaking his head. "Oh, Gigi, if you only knew how I have hoped."

"But I know Mimi. She must hope."

His hands lifted briefly from the wheel. It was obvious that he didn't want to talk about it any more.

Gigi made an attempt to concentrate on what she was able to see, making comparisons with what she knew of rural America. The people here might be poor, but she saw no shacks, no ugliness of architecture, no billboards, no dooryards cluttered with worn-out cars. The few houses, close to the edge of the road, all had a look of ancient dignity. They were built of stone; the pale roofs had little tufts of plants growing here and there between the tiles.

Almost every house had a dog that rushed out, barking, and a walled grove of orange and lemon trees, leaves shining blackly, the jeweled fruit so heavy that in places it bent the branches to the ground.

Richard gestured toward a mist of white ahead of them, not the first she had noticed. "Almond blossoms, Gigi. They're at their height right now. Somebody wrote a poem once that compares Majorca at almond-blossom time to a basket of flowers floating on the sea. Some are white, some are pink, as you shall see by day."

She inhaled their loveliness in the sharp night air, sweet, with a sadness that seemed enhanced by the light of a moon that was almost full. If, she thought, I could only have seen Mimi one more time with that vibrant gaiety that seemed never to change from one summertime to the next, as if she had thought that summer would go on endlessly. She knew that she might have taken a word of warning from that last letter mentioning the doctor's admonitions to rest. But Mimi had covered it all so quickly with gaiety about her laziness, her vanity, that those few words had made no impression.

"Richard, did she get my last letter?"

"Yes. It came just two or three days ago."

"I hope I didn't say anything to upset her."

"I think she was a bit concerned that you seemed to be delving into the past, worrying over things that are best forgotten."

"If you think I shouldn't mention any of that, I'll avoid it."

"It's foolish for you yourself to worry about it. I was there, as you may have been told, and remember it all. You were too young, I'm sure."

"I remember nothing. Did you read my letter?"

"No. Mimi told me about it."

Gigi wondered just how much Mimi had told him. "Are there—have there ever been—witches on this island?"

"If one wants to believe the old wives' tales, yes. Valldemosa—we'll not go through it now, but it's to our left—is said to have had more than its share of witches at one time."

"Valldemosa—that's where Chopin . . . ?"

"Right-o. He was there, you know, with the French baroness, the writer who called herself George Sand."

She nodded. "One of the first of the women libbers. Wore pants, smoked cigars or cigarettes."

"Yes. Lived in open sin with him in a monastery which had recently been deserted by the monks. Quite a scandal to the villagers, and that book she wrote, calling them thieves and savages, didn't help any." He glanced at her, smiling. "I rather think my Mimi fancied herself another George Sand when we came here. Not that she could ever have been a writer, poor darling. Not that, by then, living in sin was any great shakes."

"Do you believe there is any such thing as a witch?"

"No. I'm rather a pragmatic fellow, I'm afraid. Chopin may have believed in them. He wrote many compositions which bore the name of Valldemosa, and in some of them, if one uses a bit of imagination—of which I'm sure you have a great deal—one is supposed to be able to hear witches crying. I'll put some of his music on the hi-fi for you at the house and you can make up your own mind about it."

Gigi wasn't sure she wanted to listen to that music.

"But then, Chopin was a fanciful fellow. He was very ill while he was at the monastery, and had a premonition that he would die there—which, like most premonitions, didn't come true. In one of his pieces can be heard the slow, marching tread of those who carried his coffin along the corridor. Then one hears the thud of the coffin as it is dropped into the tomb, the sound of earth as it falls on the coffin lid." Richard flashed her a glance. "How did I get off on all this? Oh, yes, your question about witches. I know why you're interested, of course. Mimi told me about that bit in your letter."

She made no reply, didn't feel like discussing it right now with Richard. Later, after she had talked to Mimi, she might be willing, even relieved, to be able to discount the words she had said twice under hypnosis.

"Back to Chopin for a moment. He turned to religion, embraced the Church while he was here, rather than his erstwhile love. I do not pretend to be a religious man, but bear with me, it's the mood I'm in tonight. I can understand how when a man loses his love he can turn to religion. It

86

has happened so many times. Another man who did that was Ramón Llull, one of the saints of the island." He broke off, gave Gigi an apologetic smile. "When I get started on island stories, I'm afraid I get to be an awful, crashing bore. Hasn't Mimi ever told you that I become infatuated with the sound of my own voice?"

"No, never. Please don't worry. Just go on."

"Actually, I'm not too apologetic, as I feel that any visitor to Majorca should be told about Ramón Llull. He's been dead now about seven hundred years and he was probably the most remarkable man this island ever produced. A great writer, educator, traveler, hermit, mystic. I'm sure the name is familiar to you . . ."

"No." Gigi shook her head, hoping the admission wouldn't make her appear too ignorant.

"The thing that most intrigues me about him was that in his early days he was quite a rounder. He was the rich, indulged son of a nobleman, and used to having his way with any woman of his choice. But he fell in love with a beautiful girl who was pure and devout. He wooed her ardently, writing poems to her breasts, and all that sort of thing. Nothing he could do would induce her to look at him. So this exhibitionist of a fellow—not unlike me, I rather see myself doing such a thing in my younger days—rode his horse up the steps of the church where she was praying, openly declaring his love before all the worshipers. Imagine his joy when she sent her duenna—or so one version of the story has it—to tell him to come to her house. He thought he had won her. Imagine his passion as she began to loosen her gown over her breasts. And then"—Richard's voice dropped and he looked toward Gigi—"imagine his horror when he saw that one of the beautiful breasts he had admired was being eaten with cancer. That was when he turned to the Church. The girl's name was Ambrosia, which I find rather charming. I also like his philosophy: 'He who loves not, lives not.' " His voice, beautifully modulated, invested the words with sad meaning.

Wistfully, Gigi said, "I think it may be true." And then, "You should have been an actor."

He laughed. "I'm a ham. Just give me an audience. Actually, I was an actor until I got this bum knee. Mimi may have told you."

"No." Beyond the fact that she adored him and didn't want to risk marriage spoiling their relationship, Mimi had told her almost nothing about him. But Gigi didn't want to say that. "Tell me some more about Majorca. I didn't have a chance to study before I came, and I know very little about it. I'm so bad at geography that I have only a vague idea where the island's located. Off the coast of Spain, in the Mediterranean, but . . ."

He gave her an amused smile. "You're like the girl told about by one of our delightful island writers, Robert Graves. This girl said, when asked where Majorca was, 'I don't know. I flew.' "

"That's me, I'm afraid."

"Well, to put it into miles for you rather than kilometers, we are about a hundred miles east of the Spanish peninsula. At the moment we are driving north. Just ahead of us is Son Baraitx, our nearest village."

"How much further to the house?"

"About three miles. The village has been declared a national monument, which means that one must get permission from the powers that be to alter so much as a door knocker. No high-rises ever, thank God. Since last month's storm knocked out our telephone wires, we've had to come here when we wanted to use the phone. Occasionally we pick up a few groceries, but the one store here charges such high prices that Concepción usually takes the truck to the Saturday market in Palma each week. A very big deal for her and she is apt to make a day of it."

"Concepción?"

"Our servant. Things have been a bit tight with us and she's the only one left. Devoted to Mimi. She has been with us ever since we came here, but you probably don't remember her."

"No. But I do, very vaguely, remember Catalina, the one who took me back to the States. I'd like to look her up."

"Do you remember her last name?"

Gigi shook her head. "It's probably changed by now—she must be married."

"Then it may not be easy to find her, since half the girls in the village seem to have that name, Catalina Tomas being one of the island's favorite saints. According to island legend, as an infant, some four hundred years ago, she was so precocious and holy that she refused to take milk from her mother's breast on Fridays. I'm not asking you to believe that."

"I'd find it hard. I find it hard to believe that people anywhere still believe in things like that."

"Here, some of them do. It's not for me, but perhaps such simplicity is to be envied. Another story that they tell about this same Catalina has to do with a time when she was carrying food to workers in the field. When she fell and broke the vessel and lost the food, she said the devil threw her. Whereupon the angels, mind you, took over the show, mended the vessel, and served a sumptuous heavenly meal."

Gigi was looking toward a dark village that climbed the hill to their right.

"That's Son Baraitx. We can come here to inquire sometime about your Catalina, but right now, as you can see, the village is sleeping."

They left the main highway. The road now was rough, with no guardrails on either side although some of the drops were horrendous. Richard drove with skill, but recklessly, it seemed to Gigi. She clung to the little shelf in front of her.

"Am I frightening you, little Gigi? Don't be frightened. I know this road so well, potholes and all, and I have such confidence in my superb driving—boastful, but true—that you're safer than you'd be back home on any of those freeways I've heard so much about. Watch now for the sea on our left."

In another minute, there it was, the Mediterranean. Calm and dark except for the moon path and the white froth of waves which crashed on the rocks edging the shore.

Gigi said, breathless, "Oh, how you must love all this!"

"I do. I love all of Spain. I became a citizen years ago, that's how I feel about it. And the best place of all—well, look up there, just ahead." He was slowing, bringing the little Seat to a halt. "I always stop right here and force new arrivals to admire."

A great sprawling pile of stone stood silhouetted in the moonlight, straggling upward, seemingly perched on the very edge of the cliff. On the end nearest them, a tower stood, square and tall, topped with square spaced stones.

Awed, Gigi said, "I've seen pictures, but they never did it justice. I never dreamed—Mimi never said—she owned a castle."

"Oh, it's not. It's only a *quinta*—that's from the Arabic and it means country house. It was started as a simple farmhouse back in the twelfth century, as nearly as we can discover, and over the centuries various owners have just kept adding on. The tower is quite new, only four hundred years old."

"That doesn't seem new to me."

"It was added when Barbary pirates were raiding the coast. There are the arrow slits, a bit hard to see in this light. Similar towers were built all along the coast, and from the tops of them they used to signal the approach of the pirate ships. The towers were miles apart, but the torches were visible by night and the smoke by day. I think I may have missed my time by a few centuries. I'm a romantic at heart, Mimi tells me. But can't you just imagine how exciting it all must have been?"

"Yes, yes."

"My Ca'n Cornitx. I love it. I love it."

Gigi was moved by the intensity of his voice.

In low gear, they finished the climb. Only a few lights were visible in the windows, dotted here and there. The house faced the sea. They drove along the back of the tower, past a dimly lit service entrance where a truck was parked. They swept up around the other end of the house and down around to the front on a wide graveled driveway.

"Here we are," Richard said, his smile boyish now, his tone light. "Welcome to Ca'n Cornitx."

9

S*he* saw a wide doorway, lighted on either side by antique lanterns, electrified. Red geraniums, gorgeous in
full bloom, stood tall beside the arched double doors, the
worm-eaten wood heavily banded with iron.

Richard got out, took her bag, and lifting a massive latch,
swung one of the great doors open onto a tiled *entrada*
where a fountain in the center splashed into a shallow stone
basin. A variety of green plants stood everywhere, some of
them in big *ollas* that looked as if they could have been
brought up from the sea, relics of Roman or Grecian ship-
wrecks. Two staircases curved upward gracefully.

Richard gestured to the right, his eyes on the girl's face,

as if enjoying her expression of wonder. Gigi put one hand on the wrought-iron railing, suddenly finding that she dreaded the moment of confrontation with the ailing Mimi.

The door at the top opened. A woman stood there. She wore a black dress and white apron, and the Junoesque figure and mature handsomeness seemed for a moment familiar to Gigi.

"Concepción, of course. Do you remember her?"

"No. But she looks familiar somehow. Perhaps like someone I've seen." Gigi smiled at the woman as she mounted the stairs toward her. *"Buenas noches."*

"Buenas noches, señorita." The woman inclined her head, but she did not return the smile. Her black hair was braided, wound into a coronet on top of her head. She reached for the bag, pushed open another heavy door.

They entered a very large salon. The fire blazing in a massive fireplace at one end was a magnet. Gigi went toward it. She said to Concepción, *"Dónde está . . . ?"* She could not remember the word for grandmother.

Richard said a few words to Concepción, who answered briefly. He turned to Gigi. "She has retired, my dear. Unfortunately, you won't be able to see her tonight. I should have told you that she'd probably not be able to wait up. I must also tell you that you won't be able to converse much with Concepción. She speaks no English, can speak Spanish, but prefers mostly the Majorcan, quite a separate language, derived from the Catalan, and delivered always in very loud, rather nasal, tones, which you will soon become aware of. I've picked up a smattering of it, just enough to get by, though I can't bring myself to shout the way they do."

"I wouldn't say she seems exactly pleased to see me." She kept her voice low, just in case Concepción might be able to pick up a few words.

"Her manner is a little stiff, but I assure you she's a jewel. Do warm yourself there. I'll get us some sherry. We must talk for a bit."

He followed Concepción through a door that led toward the rear of the house. Gigi looked around, her back toward the welcome fire. Red velvet draperies hung at the deep-silled windows that overlooked the sea. Opposite the windows, curving stairs led upward to a narrow balcony. The furniture was mostly Spanish antique, heavily carved, with comfortable sofas and chairs. White plastered walls held several tapestries, flat carvings of dark wood and numerous gilt-framed oil paintings.

Gigi moved about the room, looking curiously at some of the paintings. A light-skinned serving girl with Mamie Eisenhower bangs and a see-through blouse proffered a bowl of fruit to a trio of dark-skinned, leering kings. A dwarf, grossly misshapen, seemed to provide amusement for a group of children, one of whom held a whip. A dour, middle-aged Virgin held her spouting breast to the mouth of the Child, who resembled a wooden doll. In spite of the strange subject matter of some of the paintings, most of them gave the impression of brightness and cheer with their light Spanish reds. The same red was repeated in a huge arrangement of flowers on a long table under the balcony.

Gigi moved back to the fire. The room was in beautiful order, as if ready for a party. But the party, she thought sadly, was over. She had come too late.

Richard returned with glasses and a decanter, together with some biscuits on a silver tray. He poured the dark topaz liquid into stemmed crystal glasses and handed one of them to her, raising her own. "*Salud.*"

"*Salud.*" She sipped the sherry, a little too sweet for her taste, but good, with a rich, nutty flavor.

"Forgive me, child. I should have asked if you were hungry. Concepción has gone to take your bag up to your room, but when she comes down she can so easily prepare—"

"No, no, I'm not hungry, Richard. I ate on the plane." It had been an unappetizing meal, hours ago, but she still was not hungry. "I am disappointed not to see Mimi, at least for a moment. Are you sure she's asleep?"

"Quite. The pain, you see, makes quite a bit of sedation necessary."

Gigi set down her glass. This was the first time she'd had an opportunity to study his face. His smile was gravely sweet. He was pale, as if he didn't have much time to be outdoors. He had, she decided, a romantic, Byronic look, with a high forehead, slightly receding hairline, and a mane of graying hair that was, in the back, about the length of her own. She had been prepared for Continental sophistication, brilliance. But in addition, Richard Trevelyan-Jones was—she searched her mind—dear.

His eyes, now fixed on hers, held sadness, then, suddenly, tears. He turned away, took out his handkerchief and blew his nose. "Forgive me. I still can't get used to the idea that she is . . ."

"Richard, I know. Neither can I. I have only her and she has only me." She stopped, realizing that was tactless. "As blood relations, I mean. I know what you and Mimi have meant to each other all these years."

"We have had a wonderful life, yes. I would have married her long years ago—if that matters to you. But she always felt, my funny little darling, that legal ties would somehow spoil things. Bless her heart, she clung so passionately to unconventionality long after it had ceased to matter."

"I asked you this once, but do you suppose she admits to herself how sick she is?"

"I suppose she must. We've not discussed it. One doesn't, somehow, with a person like Mimi."

"In the morning—— Richard, I can't help dreading it. I won't know what to say to her."

He lifted his hands, palms up, let them fall. "Well, you are here, that's what matters. Tell me, now that you're here, don't you remember any of this?"

Gigi looked around the room, shaking her blond head slowly. "I don't. I don't remember anything."

"You should. You played here often enough, charmed our guests, sat on laps, listened to watches ticking. Oh, you were an enchanting infant." He raised his glass, giving a nod in her direction. "Still are enchanting. But what about me—now that we've talked for a bit, don't you remember me at all?"

"No. But, Richard, I was only—"

"Dickie—that's what you used to call me. A pet name Mimi had for me. I'll admit it caused me to cringe a bit."

"It doesn't suit you."

"I'm glad." He glanced at the tall clock that ticked on one wall. It was close to midnight. "You must be very tired."

"I didn't get much sleep on the plane, but I keep reminding myself that it's early at home."

"Well, I'm sure you would like to go up to your room now. Maybe the room where we have put you will bring back some memories. That is, unless you'd like a drop more of the sherry?"

Gigi found his pronunciation of the word sherry—almost "sheddy"—very charming. She got up. "No more, thank you. Where are you going to put me?"

"Come and I'll show you."

He went to lift heavy portieres aside from one of the many doors, opened the door, and she saw a long corridor, turning, the walls roughly plastered. The floor was stone. Gigi drew her coat about her; it was cold and drafty here. They passed several doors, and at the end of the long passage, they came to another door. He pushed it open. They stepped down, outside now in a large flagstoned courtyard with the walls of the tower extending upward around them.

Except for the fact that it was square, the enclosure seemed a little bit like a huge midwestern silo. A primitive well was in the center. The ground level was open to the back, and workbenches extended along the other three sides.

Richard paused. "In our early days here, this is where the servants would prepare the food—wash the vegetables, pluck the chickens, do whatever it is they do to pigs and goats—for the big parties we used to have. It was nothing for us to have fifty or more guests. Over there"—he pointed —"is the spit where the meat was roasted. Ah, we lived like kings in those days, Gigi. And I must say I don't regret a moment of it."

"I wish I could have been here then."

"You were, of course, though you don't remember. Up there is the room that will be yours while you are here."

Gigi looked at him in surprise. "The tower room—that's where my mother and I . . ."

"Yes." He was gesturing toward steps that zigzagged upward, with a railing along the front wall. "It's not the oldest part of the house, but it's the most romantic. It's the favorite spot for all our guests, and as you will see, it's fixed for comfort. When we came, it was fit only for the pigeons. I did most of the work there myself and I'm proud of it. A nimble child like yourself won't mind the steps, I hope. There are forty-eight of them."

"Oh, I won't mind the steps, Richard, but you needn't bother to come up." To her relief, he brushed aside her protest.

"Oh, yes, I want to come up this one time and make sure that you are nicely settled and that Concepción hasn't forgotten anything you may need. Note the arrow slits in the walls as you go up."

Noting the arrow slits, Gigi took the steps slowly, out of consideration for his bad knee. But she was out of breath by the time they reached the top.

On the outside of the door, he touched a large bolt and looked around at her with a smile. "Let me call your attention to this—you might not have noticed. It's just another little charming story that goes with the house. A jealous wife once locked her philandering husband in here to teach him a lesson. He was a shadow of himself when she let him out, after starving him for a week. I believe they lived happily ever after. That's one of the stories that tickles Mimi's fancy. She tells it to every guest. She's kept me on short leash, I can tell you, all these years. Not that I've minded. The milk-and-water type never has had any appeal for me."

With a flourish then, he opened the door and stood back. The big, square room was almost Spartan in its simplicity, with pale tiled floor, rough white plaster on the walls, and a heavily beamed ceiling that arched between each beam. On the carved wooden bed she saw a homespun woolen spread in a bright Majorcan design of red, blue, and yellow. Draperies of the same material hung at the windows. Judging from the deep sills, the walls up here must be four feet thick. Large sheepskins lay here and there on the uneven tiling of the floor.

She looked around. "It's strange not to have some glimmer of memory after staying here all those months. It may come back, I suppose."

"Yes." He gave a pat to her shoulder. "We'll talk about that in a minute." He crossed to the corner fireplace where a small fire burned. "Concepción, I see, has made you rather a stingy little fire—typical of these islanders who aren't used to the comfort Americans require. But there are plenty of these slabs of olive wood in that basket. Do use as much as you wish. It's very heavy, lasts a long time, and is our favorite wood for burning."

He limped across to a door, which he opened. "This is the bath. You can light the Butano in there if you should need it. Right next to it we have—*voilà!*" He threw open double doors and stood back, looking around for her approval.

Gigi saw that on one side her clothes had been hung neatly on hangers. On the other side a modern dressing table had lights all around the mirror, Hollywood-style. On the small floor, deep shag carpeting, bright red, made it as gaily modern as if it had come from the pages of a magazine.

"Rather an anachronism, but the ladies seem to like it. Concepción had to rush to get everything ready, but I hope you will find what you need."

"I'm sure. It's lovely, Richard. Flowers, even . . ." On the desk by the front windows, a bouquet matched the yellow in the Majorcan fabric.

"I'm glad you noticed. I told Concepción to put them here. Her arrangement leaves something to be desired." He pulled the branches into a more pleasing shape so that the little ball-shaped blossoms fell gracefully.

"I've seen that in florists' windows, but what is it?"

"Mimosa. Sunny flowers for welcome on a cold, sad night. *No es verdad?*"

"*Sí, señor. Muchas gracias.*"

"*De nada.*" He gave a deprecatory wave. At the front, he drew the curtains back from the floor-length windows, looked out for a moment. "It was a hasty decision, putting you here. I hope it was the right one. Mimi has read me your letters over the years. I think I know you pretty well, little Gigi. In your last one you said that you needed to get back."

"Yes. Back to the love."

"Here in this room I hope you may be able to do just that. I think I understand you better than some people would. My own parents were killed by a bomb at the very end of World War I. I was only a few months old. They left no money. I was raised on the cold, grudging charity of relatives." Bitterness came to his eyes. "It leaves its mark."

She felt a wave of empathy, wanted to take the bitterness from his eyes. Softly, she said, "I'm glad you've had Mimi." The age difference, she thought. He may have been searching for a mother. Mimi wasn't old enough to be his mother, but she hoped that she had been able to supply some of his needs.

As if he read her mind, he said, "Mimi has made up for everything. Few men are as lucky as I have been." He came across the room, took her face in his hands. "*Buenas noches,* sweet child. I do hope I haven't kept you up too long with my talking."

"I needed to talk. Thank you, thank you for everything, Richard." She cocked her head. "Dickie . . . ?"

"Never mind. As I told you, I never liked it." He kissed her warmly on both cheeks.

She said, "In the morning—I know my Mimi—she'll want plenty of time to make herself look pretty. How soon should I . . . ?"

"Oh, not early. Get a good rest. I hope you will sleep as late as you can."

"Richard, I've not given up. I still hope that things aren't as bad for her as you say."

"Don't hope. In the morning you'll know what I mean. But don't worry about anything now. Sleep late. Concepción will bring coffee—unless you prefer tea?"

"Coffee."

"Very good, I'll tell her. I'll also tell her to bring you some of that marvelous pastry—the *ensaimadas*—that they make on this island. You have fruit there by your bedside."

Gigi turned to look, saw a bowl of little oranges on her bedside table.

"The Continental breakfast may not be enough for you. You can have something more hearty if you prefer. Bacon and eggs—perhaps an omelet?"

"Oh, no. At home I eat scarcely any breakfast. Whatever Concepción brings me will be fine. Why don't I just come down? Those steps are—"

"Not at all. Lock your door from the inside with the key if it makes you feel better. But Majorca is one of the few safe places left in the world."

"I'm not afraid."

He turned back when he reached the door, then looked at her with that smile that seemed so much to want her to like him. "I'm so glad we're friends. I've always known we would be."

When she had taken a relaxing bath in the cheerful little bathroom with its white walls and red towels, she drew back the heavy Majorcan spread, turned down the bed. The sheets were linen, hemstitched and monogrammed. They smelled as if they might have been stored with some fragrant, unfamiliar herb. Everything was unfamiliar to her. She glanced toward the window that had the balcony outside. In the morning she would get up her courage to go out there and look down to the rocks where her mother . . .

Don't think of that now. Richard had had his reasons for putting her in this room. Perhaps because he knew, as Joshua knew, that a realistic confrontation with past sorrows would be a healing thing. Here in this room she might be able to get back to the love.

She turned out the light, but instead of getting into bed she went to sit in the bentwood rocker, her bare feet cozy on the white sheepskin warmed by the fire. She must have sat here in this rocker on her mother's lap many times, perhaps looking into a fragrant olive-wood fire such as this.

She rocked gently. In her grandfather's house there had been a fire sometimes in the library grate. She used to lie in front of it and look into the embers, imagining small castles, miniature scenes. Once, she remembered, a spurt of blue flame had looked like a little figure, dancing and waving, in a blue dress. She had woven a fanciful story about the little girl, imagined that she called, "Come in, come in to my snug little house. Make yourself smaller, smaller, until you can walk through the soft, warm ashes."

She had let herself be hypnotized, strange, suggestible child that she was, and imagined that she walked into that little golden house. A fantasy, dear and attractive, that she could escape the coldness of that big house on the bluff. Get away from the brown leather and gray rugs and fumed oak and Grandfather's gray mustache over the mouth that almost always opened to say, "No," then closed into that straight line again.

Oh, my mother, did you never guess what a lonely child I would be?

The embers fell, dying. She could not make anything out of them. She must get into bed before the room became cold. She drew the sheet over her, both of the white woolen blankets.

In the night she dreamed. A young child was crying. She opened her eyes, seemed to hear it, lay there listening. She closed her eyes, turned over. The lonely sound of the crying child fitted into her dreams.

10

Slow steps on the stairs told Gigi that her breakfast was arriving.

"Come in . . ." She had not locked the door. "*Entre, por favor.*"

Concepción came in with a tray; she set it down, flashing a somber look toward the bed. "*Buenos días, señorita.*" She was breathing heavily from the climb, and as Gigi returned the greeting she wondered if the woman was cross because of the extra tasks imposed upon her.

Concepción drew the draperies wide on a gray morning, then knelt at the corner fireplace to make a tepee of the olive-wood slabs, using thin bamboo sticks for kindling.

"*Gracias, Concepción. Cómo está la señora—uh—esta mañana?*"

A torrent of words, fast and loud and undistinguishable.

"*Yo no sé.* I am sorry—*lo siento.*" Gigi spread her hands apologetically.

Concepción repeated the words more loudly, as if she thought the girl had a hearing problem. "*El señor—Don Ricardo.*"

"Oh, yes, *sí.* I will ask *el señor. Gracias, Concepción.*"

Gigi sat before the newly kindled fire, grateful for its warmth as she ate the sheer, crumbling pastry that left a dusting of powdered sugar on her fingers. These must be the *ensaimadas* that Richard had mentioned; there were two of them, large, flat, so delicious that she could have eaten more. The coffee was good, hot and very strong. A small fruit knife lay with the bowl of little oranges, hardly necessary for peeling the thin-skinned fruit. She ate one, then another, sweeter and more tender than any she had ever tasted.

It was now almost nine o'clock. The Spanish instructions for lighting the small Butano heater in the bathroom were hard to make out, but with the help of her dictionary-phrase book she managed to get it going. She washed, then dressed in the pale-blue sweater and slacks that she had worn the night she went to The Smokehouse with Josh. Later it would be all right to wear the comfortable old jeans she had brought, but on this first morning she wanted to please Mimi with the way she looked.

As she slipped her feet into rubber-soled loafers, she reflected that Mimi never had lectured her on morals or health or any of the other subjects that a grandmother might concern herself with, but only on appearance and other matters equally superficial. That had been during the bad year when she had lived with a group of her rootless contemporaries.

Mimi had been charm itself to them and they had loved her, but to Gigi she had said, "Sandalwood incense? It smells more like old sandals burning! These flower children —whoever thought to call them that, with their frazzled, unwashed hair, bare, dirty feet? I adore them all, but must they fake poverty, make such a cult of ugliness? Girls, my Gigi, are supposed to *try*. Your hair must always *shine*. Do try to find yourself a decent hairdresser, darling."

Gigi picked up her brush and gave several strokes to her hair, remembering that she had astonished her grandmother by saying she didn't know anybody who went to a hairdresser. She leaned toward the mirror to apply a shimmer of pale-blue eye shadow, some dark mascara to her lashes. The faint smile of reminiscence disappeared. Had her mother looked into this mirror on those last days with anguish, despair, or only the calm decision of a depressed mind to seek release on the rocks below?

She forced herself to open the window then, step out onto the balcony, look down over the railing at the pitiless, jagged rocks. Mist, mercifully, softened them a little. Gray pigeons flapped upward, the mist seeming to muffle the sound of their wings, their mournful cooing. She lingered only a few seconds. She was relieved to have this moment of confrontation over, relieved also that no memories of that broken body—she must have seen it—had come back.

Richard had been wise to put her in this room. Their similar childhoods were a bond between them. Josh Lincoln, for all his understanding, could not quite match the firsthand knowledge of an unloved child.

A few drops of rain. Back in her room, she picked up her breakfast tray to save steps for Concepción, and began a careful descent of the rather uneven zigzagging steps. She would not try to find the kitchen, and was not sure that she wouldn't take a wrong turn along the passage that led to the salon.

She opened one wrong door and found herself in what looked as if it could be the servants' dining room. She backed out, followed the gray, cheerless passage until she reached the warmth and color of the big room where she and Richard had sat the night before.

He was there with Concepción. They were talking together and did not hear her rubber-soled approach.

She called a cheerful *"Buenos días!"*

Concepción came quickly to relieve her of the tray.

Richard returned her greeting. "You need not have bothered with the tray, but I am sure Concepción is grateful. We were just talking about you, wondering how soon you would feel like coming down. You are looking very fresh and rested, I must say. Very pretty."

"Thank you. How is Mimi this morning? I tried to ask Concepción earlier, but we don't communicate very well. Is Mimi ready to see me yet? What did she say when you told her I had come?"

"Sit down over here by the fire. It's beastly outside this morning. I just noticed a few drops of rain. I'm sure it will start pouring at any moment. Pity, when the almond blossoms are just at their height. I'm so glad I brought that mimosa in when I did. Oh, I promised you some Chopin, didn't I?"

He had been about to join her by the fire, but now he went to the hi-fi, selected some records, and in a moment the sounds of one of the preludes filled the room. "This is one of those he wrote while at Valldemosa. Poor, sick, unhappy Frederick. Strange, you know, that he never dedicated a single one of his compositions to the woman who shared his bed for so many years."

Gigi wasn't much interested right now in hearing about the loves and sorrows of two who had died well over a century ago, but he went on. "His *Berceuse* is said to be based on an old Majorcan lullabye. Listen for it—I think it's in this stack."

He moved his hand to the sound of the music as he came back across the room. He opened a silver case. "Cigarette?" The ruby on his hand caught the light. "Oh, I forgot. You don't smoke."

"I'll have one." Something about his manner made her want to have something to hold. She backed up a little closer to the fire. The record had changed now, was doleful, depressing. She remembered what Richard had told her about the measured tread of monks bearing a coffin.

"How about some more coffee? I could have Concepción . . . ?"

"No, thanks. I had two cups upstairs." She kept her eyes on his face.

He lit her cigarette, then went to stand by the windows, smoking and looking out at the rain. After a bit he said over his shoulder, "My dear, I suppose there is no easy way, no gentle way . . ."

Gentle? "I know how ill she is. You've already told me that. I know that I can't expect her to look the same—to *be* the same as she was last summer. Are you going to tell me that even this morning she doesn't feel well enough to see me?"

"Last night I knew how tired you were. There was no point in denying you a good night's rest. I was—you may have noticed—under a great deal of stress. You may even have guessed the truth."

"The—truth?"

"Mimi is dead, my dear. There now, it's said. Not tactfully."

She said blankly, "Dead?"

He came to put his arms about her. He patted her shoulder. "I did not know how to tell you." His voice sounded tired. "Concepción—that was what we were talking about —said I should have prepared you carefully to ease the shock. But you had to know. It seemed best just to come out with it."

"When did she die? Last night? Oh, I wish . . ." She would have turned away from him, but his arms held her.

"No, my dear, no. Last night was already too late. She had died the day before."

"The day before yesterday? But that was the day she sent the cable."

"Yes. She told me what to say. I telephoned the cable from the little store in Son Baraitx, not knowing the end was so near. Nor, I'm sure, did she. I came back to tell her I had sent the cable, and she was very happy. She was sure you would come on the first possible plane. About an hour later she was gone."

"And the funeral, I suppose, will . . ." Her voice was lifeless.

"My dear child. Spanish law requires that burial must be within twenty-four hours. We could not wait for you. I am glad you were spared the shock of seeing the way she looked. So wasted, my poor darling. Toward the end she really hated having anyone see her. Bless her, she was so vain."

"But if somebody—you or she or somebody—had let me know sooner, I could have come at any time. Oh, Richard, it doesn't seem right that I didn't come!"

"Try to be glad you can remember her the way she was last summer."

"She was all I had. I said that last night, but . . ."

"I know. And she adored you. Look, Gigi, I can see that you're in a bit of a shock. I'm sorry I couldn't have handled things a little better. Why don't you go on up to your room for a while? I'm sure you would like to lie down."

She turned away from him, spread her arms wide, let them fall heavily against her sides. "I—I don't know what I'd like to do. I feel stunned. I can't think straight."

"That's natural."

"I feel like . . . Richard, I guess what I ought to do is get on a plane and go right back. There's no reason for me to be here now."

"No, no. I simply won't hear of that. I need you here, Gigi, that's why I didn't try to get in touch with you and keep you from rushing over. We have so many things to discuss. This has been a crushing blow to me too. I—somehow can't seem to face life without her. All these years. All these rooms in this house we've loved so much have an emptiness now that I can't quite believe."

He turned his head away, but Gigi saw the glint of tears. She put her arms around him, leaned her head against his shoulder. "I know. I'm sure I know. Forgive me for thinking only of myself there for a bit. And thank you for letting me sleep last night. You were right to do everything just as you did. I suppose I should stay on. Right now, Richard, I think I'll go up to my room for a little while."

"Good girl. You'll need a bit of time to pull yourself together, not want a lot of palaver that won't do one bit of good. I'm going to ask Concepción to serve us a nice luncheon here at one. And then this afternoon I thought I would drive you to see the grave."

"Grave." She said the word dully, shaking her head.

"It's in the little cemetery of Son Baraitx. People loved her there."

"People loved her everywhere. That time she came to visit me when I was living with all those kids—she represented everything they were all rebelling against, but they loved her."

"I'm sure. An age gap, culture gap, was nothing to her. The simple people of Son Baraitx came to the little service we had yesterday. I hope you approve of her being buried here."

"Oh, yes. Where else? She would certainly not have wanted to go back to Peoria and lie beside . . ." She stopped. Again she had been tactless.

But Richard gave her a smile and a bit of a laugh. "Indeed, no. She would have haunted us both. Rather noisily, I'm afraid. It's good that we can laugh just a little, isn't it? Oh, we shared so many little jokes. That one would have appealed to her. You go on up. Luncheon here, then, at one. And after that we will go to Mimi's grave."

II

Rain fell now in slashing gusts. Richard parked the Seat on a narrow road that led to the little cemetery. It was walled, on a hill overlooking Son Baraitx. He reached to open the car door, and Gigi caught hold of his hand. "Wait. I can't. Let's not get out. I hate cemeteries. I don't want to see her grave."

"All right. Gigi, you don't have to do anything you don't want to do. But let me tell you something that I think may help you later on. We have to work our way through grief, and that's not done by avoidance of the realities of death. It hurts—God, how it hurts—but it helps to heal. Do you understand?"

"No. I—yes, maybe." That wisdom of his again.

"In times past, the last, necessary ministrations for the dead were done by the families. These days, unable to bear even the thought of approaching death, too many people whisk their dying loved ones off to hospitals. I kept my girl with me." He stopped, steadied his voice. "And when it was over, I picked out one of her favorite dresses to be buried in. It was pale coral, almost a match for that lovely hair. Cashmere, long-sleeved, high-necked. Warm. She . . . she minded the cold so much."

He had turned his face away. Gigi pressed her forehead against his shoulder for a moment. "Oh, Richard. I'll look at the grave if you want me to."

They got out. Around her, Gigi held an ugly blue plastic raincoat with torn buttonholes that Richard had borrowed for her from Concepción. They walked toward the iron grillwork of the gates. Shovels and pickaxes leaned against the wall inside, but no one was there. The gates looked as if they were locked, and she thought it was just as well. She had no wish to go any closer to that mound of sodden earth and rain-beaten flowers that Richard pointed to.

He was trying to open the gates. She said, "Please don't bother. I can see from here."

"Very well. I did think we might walk around in there for a bit. It's so beautifully kept. You need to remember that."

"Yes. I'll remember. It's—it's a nice little place, Richard. So peaceful. Nicer than the ones we have at home. I like all those stone angels."

Except for that one mound of new earth, the cemetery was tidy, with evidence of loving care. Flowering shrubs gleamed here and there through the gray of the rain. All of the gravestones had crosses. Some of them had framed pictures of the deceased. Mimi wouldn't want that. But Richard would know.

He said quietly, "I'll plant something pretty, one of the flowering island trees that she loved. Bougainvillaea, perhaps. I'll arrange for a stone. Something simple. You may have suggestions."

"No. Whatever you choose. She wouldn't want a cross. She wasn't a Catholic, as you know—or I guess not much of anything that had to do with religion." She glanced at him with a bit of a smile. "And, of course, no picture."

He nodded, returning her smile. "Just take a look at the faces on the photographs we can see from here. So solemn, as if they were already thinking of death. Can you imagine the incongruity of our Mimi's laughing face among them? That's another little joke she would have enjoyed. Oh, God, I miss her so!"

"So do I. I feel bereft. Nobody ever had a grandmother like her."

"There was never anybody like her. Brother Antonio said something like that yesterday at the simple little service we had for her here. A dear fellow. He had come to our house for drinks many times and he knew her well, knew how the villagers felt about her. They cried for her, Gigi. They brought flowers from their own little gardens. Some of them I kept—you saw them in that big bouquet in the salon. They were so much more meaningful to me than floral wreaths from city florists would have been. They expressed so much real love . . ." His voice broke.

She put her arms around him and he sobbed once out loud, a harsh and shocking sound there in the quiet of the rain. Only in the movies had she ever seen a man cry, and she felt helpless to comfort him. She put her face against his coat to hide her own lack of tears.

What is the matter with me that I cannot cry for my own grandmother?

Back at the house, with a pitcher of *sangría* on the small table in front of them, Gigi said, "Richard, is it so awful that I can't cry? That I can't believe it's true, or seem to make any connection between my funny, beautiful little Mimi and that pile of earth we saw this afternoon?"

"No, I think it's perfectly normal, under the circumstances. Nature provides some of us with an interval of shock. Then we muddle on through somehow until we get to the place where we can accept it."

"I want to talk about her. I want you to tell me all there is to tell. It won't bother you, will it?"

"No. It will help. Ever since day before yesterday I have been remembering all the good things we shared. There is a special kind of . . . almost joy . . . in grief that I don't expect you to understand yet. But I think we should talk first about practical matters. I am not much good at such things and I'd like to get them out of the way. Do you mind awfully?"

Gigi said she didn't mind.

"She left no will. Not surprising, I suppose, when one has never admitted the possibility of death. Her jewels will be yours."

"Oh, I care so little about jewels. She has already sent me several pieces—valuable, I know—which I never wear. That big diamond for Christmas . . ."

"Yes, a beautiful ring. And you must have what is left. They were family things, many of them, and I'd not feel right if they didn't go to you. Over the years she had sold some of her things. You may not have known that."

She gave a shrug of dismissal. She hadn't known, but she didn't care.

He lifted his glass, gestured with it around the room. "If there are pictures, a few *objets d'art* that you fancy, take them. The house—I'm sure this won't come as a surprise—is mine now. We owned it jointly."

Gigi said quickly, "Oh, of course. I know you have put a lot of yourself—money too—into the restoration. But can you bear to live here alone? Will you keep it?"

He looked shocked. "I'd not sell for all the money on earth, and I doubt I could find a buyer. Nobody wants these big places any more. No, I'll hang on with my dying breath. What I think I may have to do—Mimi and I had discussed doing this together—is turn it into a hotel. Not a hotel really, more like the *paradors* one sees on the peninsula."

"What's that?"

"Oh, one of the big, grand houses where they take guests. I'd never advertise. We have enough friends who would tell their friends. I visualize restoring the terraced gardens that used to slope down to the sea. Superb food, the finest wines. A constant house party—how Mimi would have loved that! We have a friend here who has just the sort of place I'd like to emulate. Very expensive, very exclusive. Guests must furnish the best recommendations before they're accepted. We'd have none of your crass, rich—sorry, love—Americans. You do know what I mean?"

"I do." She gave him a small smile. She knew also that this was one of the cherished concepts of many of the British, but this was no time to be defensive. "I think it's a super idea. Are there a few ghosts?"

"What do you want me to say?"

"Say yes. Ghosts are a romantic asset in a house like this."

"Good girl. After my own heart. I'd have been disappointed if you hadn't said yes, although I might have denied it if I thought you'd be frightened. I have heard some sounds at night that I couldn't ever track down. But in

England we rather accept the idea of haunted houses. Any house this old, where for centuries people have lived and died . . ."

"Some of them violently, I'm sure. I have heard—I'm not into this stuff much—but I've heard that those are the ones who come back. They are supposed to linger, especially if there is . . . unfinished business. My mother . . ."

"Poor Ann. Let's not talk about her."

"Richard, I need to talk about her. Do you mind very much? I am hoping that while I am here I will get a feeling of her presence, her love."

"She loved you very much."

"But not enough to stay." She said it wistfully.

"And you blame her for that?"

"No. Well, yes, I suppose I do."

"Nonsense." He said it briskly, poured himself some more *sangría*. She covered her glass with her hand when he held the pitcher toward her. "She was grief-stricken over your father's death. Extremely depressed. Not accountable."

"Mimi said as much. But I have tried to think that perhaps she didn't do it deliberately, that somebody—"

"No. Absolutely no way. Are you sure you want to talk about it?"

"Yes. Mimi told me so little. You tell me."

"Mimi and our three guests were playing bridge right here in this room. All the servants—we had several then— were out in the courtyard, getting ready for the big party we were planning to have that night. I had a small boat then and was just tying it up when I heard the scream. I finished securing the boat and came running."

"You don't think someone could have escaped down the stairs?"

"Past the servants? No. Matter of fact, they didn't even hear her scream. You'd understand that if you'd ever heard a bunch of them shouting and laughing together. But when the word came, Catalina, your nurse, who had been helping the others, ran up the stairs. She found the door locked from the inside."

"Why had my mother locked the door? Was she afraid of someone?"

"Possibly. Paranoid fears often exist in a disturbed mind."

Gigi nodded, sighing. "So I guess you broke in the door . . ."

"Yes. You were in your crib, crying, all alone in the room."

"Then I never saw my mother's body down on the rocks. I'm glad. But, Richard, I must have seen something— somebody—in that room!"

"Oh, Gigi, Gigi. Back to the hypnotic regression again, eh? I wish you'd try to forget about that. The subconscious is a can of worms that most of us do well to keep the lid on. I mean, what one of us dares probe old nightmares for meaning? I'm sure that's what you had. Even babies dream —I think the experts agree on that. I'd not be surprised if you'd been told the island myth that there is a witch who comes for naughty children."

"Well, I don't remember and I don't even have a clear recollection of what went on during hypnosis. I was terribly frightened and that's about all I know."

"This fellow who hypnotized you—was it somebody who knew what he was doing?"

"The second time, yes. He doesn't pretend to be an expert, but he is very responsible and has a lot of respect for the uses of hypnosis."

Richard was giving her a skeptical look. Gigi had no

wish to try to convince him of something that now had been pushed to the back of her mind as unimportant. "Back to Mimi now—she's the one we should be talking about. Before she died, did she say anything about me?"

"Yes. You remember I told you that I had just come back from sending the cablegram. She said, 'I can't wait to see my little Gigi.' She was holding my hand. And then her fingers . . . her fingers just relaxed, as if she were too tired to hold on any longer. Her eyes closed. I thought she just needed to rest. I said, 'Sleep now, darling.'" His voice was husky. "It was over. We'd had such a good life together."

"I know, I know."

"But not peaceful." He forced a smile. "No, not peaceful. She was a fiery, spirited little thing—the only sort of woman I could have loved all those years. Twenty-three of them, imagine! The fights we had—oh, classic, beautiful! In the great tradition. If I could ever get our love affair on film, I'd have a smash hit. Once I announced that I was leaving her. I was just going out the door of the *entrada* when she grabbed a plant—potted vine, some damned thing—and threw it at me. By the time I got the bloody thing unwound, we were both laughing and ended up in each other's arms. And another time she grabbed the fire tongs—those heavy things right over there—and gave me a crack across the kneecap. I'm sure she never told you about that."

Shocked, Gigi said, "No, never."

"Ah, yes. Bless her, I'm sure she didn't mean to hit so hard. It put a tidy end to my dream of being a swashbuckling lead, I can tell you that." He was smiling, a fond look in his eyes. "Can't even remember what that fight was all about, we had so many. But the reconciliations, those are what I remember, not that you could ever put them on film. Still, these days, I suppose you could."

"You could do it lovingly."

"Yes. It would be done with love. But I'll have to wait for a while, let things fall into place. You know, I just thought of one of her favorite sayings, 'Everything happens for the best.' If it hadn't been for the smashed knee, I'd never have got into the other side of the business. It's turned out to be much better—not too lucrative, but much better for me than mouthing writers' lines I couldn't always believe."

"Where do you work?"

"Over on the peninsula at Almeria, on the Costa del Sol. We've got a great setup. The terrain is marvelously like yours of the Far West. We dub in the sound. Whatever artistic ability I may have had has long since been prostituted to the lure of the quick peseta. *Que lástima*—no, it's not sad, at that. What I've made there has been able to keep the show on the road here."

"Mimi must have hated economizing."

"She never knew she had to. I kept it from her." He poured some more of the red liquid into his glass, gestured toward her, but she shook her head. She didn't care much for the fruity, winy, sweet stuff.

He finished his drink and got up. "I'm glad we'll have plenty of time to talk. Do you have to be back in Washington at any special time?"

"No, I suppose not. They can get along all right without me on my job."

"I am sure that a girl as pretty as you must have some young chap waiting."

"Just my boss. He's my best friend. That's all it is right now, just friendship. If I ever let it get going, it might turn out to be something big, kind of a lot for me to handle." She fished a cherry out of her drink, ate it looking thoughtful.

"Richard, I'm not sure I have what it takes to handle anything big. I mean, part of me just isn't there."

"Oh, balderdash. That's a word you expect us Britishers to use, isn't it? I can think of some others that might more graphically express my meaning. One of the other bits that Mimi read me from your letter just popped into my head. You said you were your own analyst. Did you ever hear the saying that anyone who is his own doctor has a fool for a doctor? I don't mean to disparage your intelligence. I certainly don't think you're a fool. I mean only that I think you should put certain events of your past behind you. It can be done. I've had to. Come now, finish your *sangría* and I'll show you the parts of the house you haven't seen."

"I've had all I want to drink. I'm dying to see the house."

"Some memories may come back."

No memories came back. He took her first to the dining hall behind the salon. It was a baronial place, with a very long table that could have seated thirty with ease. It seemed a gloomy room with its heavy, dark antiques, but she supposed that when the many silver candelabra on the table had all their candles lighted, and the place was filled with guests, it could be very festive. Several large paintings hung on the walls. The subject matter of one of them seemed hardly conducive to cheerful dining: a knight on horseback leaned, wild-eyed, as if to plunge his sword again into the side of a fallen soldier. Blood poured from the wounded man, so realistic that it looked as if it might be wet and warm to the touch.

Gigi looked away, deciding that she almost preferred the sterile still-life pictures on the dining-room walls of the house in Peoria.

"The kitchen is back through here."

They went through a butler's pantry into a brightly

lighted kitchen. It was partly ancient, with soapstone sinks and tiled walls and old copper utensils hanging; partly modern, with a huge white refrigerator and a restaurant-size stove.

Concepción looked around from the sink where she was preparing vegetables. Richard said something to her in rapid words that Gigi couldn't begin to follow. Concepción turned her handsome face to glance at Gigi in her unsmiling way, nodded, and replied in a rush of loud words that were equally impossible to understand.

"She says dinner will be served at eight. That's too early to be a very fashionable hour here, but it's not been an easy day for either of us. Will that suit you?"

"Oh, yes." They left the kitchen. "I'm not used to the time change yet. I've lost—how many hours? About five, I think, or six?"

"You can make them up with an early bedtime tonight."

Gigi touched his arm when they reached the stairs again. "I wish Concepción didn't seem so unfriendly. She scarcely looks at me."

"She is very sad. She was devoted to your grandmother. These Majorcans show their grief more readily than we do."

"Perhaps she thinks I shouldn't be smiling, chattering."

"Don't worry about it." He pointed upward. "This way for the rest of the guided tour, *señorita*."

They climbed the curving stairs. "Up here on this balcony, musicians used to sit and play for our parties. You have a vivid imagination. Can't you just visualize the scene with Mimi in the midst of it all, dancing, flirting, laughing, making everybody happy?"

"So easily, yes." But Gigi had paused before a painting that showed a scene that was anything but happy: a battleground was strewn with objects that upon close examination proved to be the parts of dismembered bodies. "The Spanish seemed to have been very bloodthirsty."

"No more so than other European people then. It was the age, a time of war and inquisition. Some rather ghastly penalties were exacted for minor infractions. For instance, a third-time cheater at cards or dice often had his fingers cut off. That seems rather much, don't you agree? A Moslem or a Jew having sexual relations with a Christian could be dismembered or tortured in any one of a number of rather grisly ways. Over there, beyond the big tapestry, you'll note a luckless fellow being burned at the stake."

"I never had any idea that Mimi's tastes ran to . . ."

"Oh, my dear, they didn't. But all the *objets d'art* were in the house when we bought it. Mimi was all for replacing what she considered gruesome with what she considered pretty. I don't know what—Degas dancers, perhaps, or sentimental scenes of lovers in a park kissing under parasols. But I finally convinced her that these paintings belonged here, were part of the history of all the centuries that this house has gone through. I rather fancy the idea that in becoming a Spanish citizen, buying this house, I have taken upon myself the sins of the past, although what we now consider sins, of course, were then only brave deeds of derring-do. I'm not a brave fellow at all. I find it much more comfortable to inhabit the twentieth century, vicariously reaping the fruits of the bravery of others who fought and slew so that I, a timid Englishman, might have this house in safety and comfort."

Gigi smiled at him with affection. He *was* a bit of a ham, with a liking for stringing words together which, delivered with his disarming candor, could easily have charmed more than this audience of one.

He opened a door at the left of the balcony. Another corridor, steps leading down, then up. Gigi saw more bedrooms than she could imagine any family would ever need.

"If I do decide to do anything commercial, I'll have to put in extra bathrooms. Proper closets, too, instead of these wardrobes and small cupboards you see in the walls. They'd hardly be adequate for the gowns my lady guests will be wearing." He apologized for the dust that lay everywhere. "We've not had guests for many months, and it seemed a needless expense to keep on the extra help necessary."

They had twisted and turned and gone up and down. Gigi said, "I feel lost, as if I should have scattered crumbs the way Hansel and Gretel did when they went into the witch's woods."

"Yes, but in this house, I fear, if you scattered crumbs, the mice would eat them."

They had come back now to the balcony. He gestured downward with his cane. But Gigi had gone past him to the door at the other end of the balcony. She opened it and looked up dark stairs to a closed door at the top. "What's up there?"

"That was used as nursery quarters many years ago by previous owners. It's total disaster now, I'm afraid." He had reached her side and was closing the door that led upward. "Do come away. You could get your head bashed in if you went up there."

"But what is . . . ?"

"It depresses me even to think of it. During our bad December storm the wind broke some of the windows. The rain came down in torrents and the plaster is falling. Part of the ceiling fell in one day when I was up there poking around. I dodged just in time. I've managed to get a man to come and board up the windows, but repairing the roof will be a major job. I keep the door up there locked in case Concepción should get some crazy idea of going in there and trying to sweep up."

As they crossed the balcony toward the stairs, they heard a noise from above. "There—did you hear that? Probably a roof tile, loosened by the rainstorm. One of those heavy tiles is enough to cause a skull fracture. Come, we'll go back downstairs now. There is a whole wing you haven't seen yet."

He took her beyond the salon. They stood at the door of the library, not entering. It was a gloomy room, heavy with the smell of old books and moldering leather, the furniture shrouded in dust covers. The music room was no more cheerful. A harp with broken strings stood in one corner. An ancient square piano was too far gone, Richard said, ever to be tuned.

Gigi pointed toward a television set. "Does it work?"

"The telly? Oh, I wouldn't know how well, love. Concepción, these last months, is the only one who's ever looked at it."

More rooms. A morning room which might be nice on a sunny day. A conservatory with many windows. Vines had climbed up over the walls, but now their withered leaves drooped. Dead plants stood around a dead fountain, the open mouths of the gargoyle heads spouting no water. Richard shook his head sadly. "Don't go in. You can imagine how this used to be."

Gigi could imagine. She had no desire to linger.

They went back toward the salon. Another of those awful paintings. A man with his head severed, blood spilling. Gigi averted her eyes, but Richard was pausing, opening a door. "This is our room—mine now, although saying it like that will take a bit of getting used to."

This room was big and square, the décor not unlike that of the tower room. A large double bed was covered with the same sort of handwoven Majorcan wool. A table held a typewriter and scattered papers and stacks of books in bright new jackets that looked as if they had just been unpacked. More books, modern-looking, filled the niches on either side of the corner fireplace. Two comfortable chairs were drawn up to a table by the windows overlooking the sea.

Gigi said, "This is nice, Richard, comfortable-looking. But it doesn't look much like Mimi."

He gave her a pleased smile. "I was waiting for you to say that. She would have been so glad to hear it. She was determined, you see, that the room should have a masculine look. She said she always pitied men who had to sleep in boudoirs of satin and lace and dotted swiss and all that frippery. She did have some of her feminine clutter in the bathroom and on that dressing table over there, but I had Concepción clear it out right away. The scent, I think, was what made me most sad—that Joy perfume she always loved. A scent, to me, is more evocative than anything else. Do you agree?"

"Yes. Some people cling, you know, leave everything as it was. Your way is best."

"I've had Concepción remove the clothes that Mimi had crammed in the closets too. At the moment, I don't know where she's put them, but you may look through them later if you like."

"Concepción can have them."

"There's a blond-mink cape—quite expensive—and some other furs."

"I'm not the type. You sell them, Richard. Keep whatever you can get for them."

"And the jewels—would you like to look through them? They're still in that wall safe over there."

"Not now. Please."

"Then come this way. I want to show you something else that guests always find interesting. The wine cellar."

Another labyrinth. They followed a passage that took them behind the kitchen, down a stairway leading to what he said was another very ancient part of the house. They entered a laundry. She saw large stone tubs and no sign of a modern appliance except for an electric iron.

They ducked under lines of clothes that hung damply, and Richard opened a door at the far end, pitch-dark, until he turned on the single bulb that hung in the middle of the room. Cobwebs were everywhere, the smell and evidence of mice. Wine racks that could have held, he told her, a thousand bottles now held only a few dozen. Great wooden casks stood against one wall.

"That's where the wine was stored before bottling. I had a go at it the first year we were here—a bloody nuisance. Wine is so cheap on this island that I prefer to buy it and by-pass all that work. And frankly, my product would not have appealed to the cultivated palate."

Brushing cobwebs off themselves, they went back through the laundry room. Richard stopped suddenly, catching her arm.

"What's the matter?" Gigi followed his eyes to a dark corner. "Not a rat. Please don't tell me . . ."

"No. Nothing, I guess. But I thought for a moment I saw our snake."

"*Snake . . . ?*"

He chuckled. "You're not afraid of them, are you?"

Gigi looked at him in astonishment. "*Richard . . .*"

"Well, don't be afraid of this one. He's an amiable chappie, perfectly harmless. Eats the rats and mice, though not all of them, I'm afraid. Concepción has made quite a pet of him."

"She would."

"I did think I should warn you. He has the run of the house."

"Great." Gigi said it faintly. "Richard, my mind tells me that a snake is more afraid of me than I am of it. And I know they don't chase people. But do you mind if we hurry on up out of here?"

When they reached the salon again, Gigi said, "Thank you for the guided tour. I'll go up now." She looked at her dusty hands. "I'll bathe, rest, maybe even nap for a while."

"Good show. I'll do the same. Now that you've seen it all, what do you think of it?"

"I think it would make a very good—whatever you said —*parador*. Give a little map, though, to your guests, or a spool of thread that they could unwind. *And* get rid of the snake."

"Ah, the feminine viewpoint, which I value most highly." He was giving her an amused look. "Mimi would have concurred most fervently. She never knew about it, since the creature arrived after she was confined to her bed. We'll lure him into a basket and convey him to some farmer's garden, although he's so attached to Concepción that he may come right back." He was teasing her. "Meanwhile, don't worry."

Gigi said she wouldn't, but she watched her steps carefully as she made her way to her room. When she had bathed, she stretched out on the bed. The room was dim with the approach of night. Back home it was still early afternoon. Josh would be on his lunch hour. She wished she could talk to him, tell him about all that had happened on this long, strange day. She was sure she could not sleep.

She slept. A little child again, she wandered through the labyrinth of rooms, trying to find her mother. *Follow her,* Concepción said to the snake, *don't let her out of your sight.* She ran, not from the snake, but from Concepción, who wore a black peaked hat. *Mommy, Mommy, where are you?*

Gigi woke to panic, disoriented in the total darkness, for several seconds unable to remember where she was. Her heart still hammering from the running in the dream, she groped for the bedside lamp, turned it on. The feeling of being lost still persisted as she looked around the room she had shared more than twenty years ago with her mother.

It was chilly now; the curtains moved a little as the wind fingered its way in around the windows. It was good of Richard, a perceptive man who seemed to understand her needs, to have put her in this place.

But no more of her mother's presence lingered here than in that brick house on the bluff in Peoria, Illinois.

12

"**P**lease tell me some more about my mother."

Concepción had served their dinner, heavy, satisfying, on a small table in front of the fire. A lighted candle provided illumination. They could have been the only guests, eating alone, in a very elegant restaurant.

Richard's deep eyes were on her face. "I have been trying to find her in you. I cannot. You have a resilience, an ability to cope, that your mother lacked. Oh, you have the same smile, I guess, the same perfect teeth."

"In the pictures of her taken here, she always had such a bright smile."

"Oh, she could turn on the smile. As if she pressed a button that had to be held to keep the light shining. But when it was released, the light went off at once. On, off. On, off. It was heartbreaking to see her."

"I wasn't enough"—she spread saltless butter on the saltless roll—"to make her want to keep the light on."

He didn't say anything, just reached for his wine.

"Richard, you and I have a lot in common. Both of us were left without parents. I'm going to be morbid—and I know you hate it—but I have read that if a child has no one to love him at a very early time in his life, that child dies."

"Depending on the child. Unless he's gutless, he manages, sometimes very well. You have survived. So have I."

"I am talking about an emotional death. I keep trying to prove that I am truly alive, capable of love."

He lifted his wineglass again, sipped, his eyes upon her. He'd had a couple of drinks before dinner that she knew of, and now inhibitions seemed to be by-passed. "Define love. Prove to me that we have, any one of the whole lot of us, much beyond the desire to please ourselves. Define love."

"You've known it."

"Indeed. Indeed I have." He touched his napkin to his lips. "Ours was one of the great loves of all time, and like other great loves, it was the perfect love-hate relationship. Does my honesty shock you? Don't look so surprised. I'd not have had it any other way. Twenty-three years of sweetness and light twenty-four hours a day! *Mon Dieu*, it would have bored the hell out of us both. But Mimi throwing things—now, that was something to see."

Gigi sipped the wine. It tasted good, but hers was not a cultivated palate. "But you knew she loved you."

"Certainly. But I also knew that she loved herself best."

She gave him another startled look, remembering that she had said those very words to Josh Lincoln.

"Don't misunderstand me. I think that's the way it should

be. We should love ourselves best. Did you ever see Mimi do her nails?"

"No, I don't think so. I always assumed that she had them done."

"She used to. Out here it wasn't always possible. Ah, it was so beautiful to see her." He said it fondly. "She gave them her entire, loving attention, polishing each one as if it were a precious jewel. And they were like jewels, oval, flawless. She loved her hair the same way, brushing it until each strand of it was like pink, shining gold. Her skin—never a night went by that she didn't go through the ritual. And her body—she knew how much I loved the youthfulness of it, how proud I was."

He had a beautifully modulated voice, not stagy, but the disciplined voice of the actor who knows the value of pauses, emphasis, little nuances of tone and expression, so that even ordinary words were invested with truth and meaning.

The spell was broken by the sound of Concepción's steps coming along the passageway from the kitchen. Gigi said, "Mr. Trevelyan-Jones, I love your voice."

"D'you like the name? I added the hyphenated bit. Jones needed a touch of class." He gave her that disarming, boyish smile. "I thought it would look good in lights. Oh, a real ham, believe me."

As Concepción cleared the table, Gigi said, "I know now why Concepción looks familiar to me. It just came to me. She looked like that Italian film star who died a year or so ago. What was her name?"

"Magnani? Anna Magnani." He glanced up at Concepción. "Yes, I think you're right, she looks like a somewhat younger Magnani."

Concepción left the room, and Richard said, "It's interesting that you should say that. I have toyed with the idea of using her in one of my films. With proper clothes, make-up, hair styling, she could probably do well enough."

"But can she act?"

"Heavens, I imagine not. It wouldn't matter. I would cast her in the role of superannuated mistress—the one who gets killed, perhaps, by the jealous wife. Or she might do even better as the jealous wife. She would simply be told to stand there, sit here, peer out from behind a curtain, plunge the dagger, whatever."

"Something sinister."

"Yes. Directing, you see, is everything. Oh, you've no idea of our low artistic level—budget level too, for that matter. Some of our actors we hire right off the streets, pay them the minimum, which they're delighted to get. All sounds are dubbed in, speech, everything. It's enormously clever how a good linguist can make the same lip movements seem to produce words that are English, French, German—you name it. Even Japanese."

"That's fascinating." She leaned her chin on her hand, under the spell of his voice again. "I've seen movies of that sort on some of the late-late shows at home. Are they commercially successful?"

"Moderately. These films are done for various foreign markets, and right now we've got a distribution problem that's giving us a bit of a hassle, but I'm sure once I can get over there, it can be straightened out."

"And you direct?"

"That and a little bit of everything else. Sometimes I dream up the plots, variations of the tried and true. Rather awful, I'm afraid, but I know which formulas work. I have a writer who turns out the scripts, simply filling in when I've blocked out the scenes that are needed to advance the story line. It's a literary version of paint-with-numbers. Rather good fun for a hack who doesn't mind prostituting his art."

Concepción returned with a silver urn of coffee and cups and saucers. "*Postre?*"

Gigi didn't know what that word meant.

"Dessert. Concepción makes a delicious *flan*—custard, I believe you say. Or you might like to try some of the marzipan roll—an almond crust rolled around candied fruits. I made a special trip to Sóller to get it for Mimi, hoping to tempt her appetite. She loves it so—loved . . ." He tapped his forehead, drew sudden breath between his teeth. "I can't seem to get used to the past tense."

"I know." Gigi put out her hand to touch his. "I don't want dessert, Richard. Just coffee."

He spoke to Concepción, quite a few words more than were needed to say, "No dessert." Gigi heard the word "cinema" and saw the quick smile on Concepción's face. She walked gracefully—perhaps exaggeratedly so—from the room, as if she were already imagining herself an actress.

Richard looked after her, laughing a little. "I told her no dessert, just leave the coffeepot here and go on to bed. That if she wanted to be a cinema star, she would need her beauty sleep."

"Do it, Richard." The girl's voice was enthusiastic. "Put her in a film if you really think it would work. She's been so faithful all these years. It can't have been a very exciting life for her living off here in this out-of-the-way place."

"Oh, I'd not waste too much pity. She's had good pay for this island. Whether we were here or not, we always kept her on full salary, and up until this last year we were here only about half the time. And I think—know, in fact —that she's found a bit of—shall we say diversion?—in the village. She was pregnant once. Mimi saw her through that and kept the very strict Catholic family from finding out about it."

He was pouring more coffee into her cup. "I hope this won't keep you from sleeping. You've not had an easy day."

"Oh, I'll sleep tonight, I'm sure of that."

But when she was up in her bed an hour later, she tossed, thumped her pillow, and could not get to sleep. It might be all that coffee, or that little nap she'd had. Or, more likely, the day had simply held too much. First the news of Mimi's death, then that dreary mound of earth seen through the wrought-iron grill. After that the tour of the house, and all the stimulating conversation with Richard that had revealed so much she never had guessed.

Had they really fought like that? It was hard—but no, not impossible—to imagine Mimi coming at him with the fire tongs. Mimi, ah, Mimi, she had been much more of a woman than those brief summer visits ever had let her granddaughter suspect.

Gigi gave up after a while and turned on the light. A glance at her watch showed her it was not quite eleven-thirty. She wished her body clock would stop telling her that at home it was early evening. She had already looked through the few books in the little niche by the fireplace. Those in English looked dull; the rest were in Spanish.

"Hey, I'm hungry." She said the words aloud and got out of bed. Surely it would be all right to go downstairs and have a prowl through the kitchen for some of that marzipan roll Richard had described so mouth-wateringly. Then in the salon she would have her choice of all the magazines she had seen there. If she was very quiet, she wouldn't disturb anyone.

The night had turned cold. She pulled on a warm robe, slipped her feet into sneakers, and made her way down the dimly lighted stone steps, across the courtyard, and along the drafty passage to the salon. It was dark now, except for the embers of the fire.

She went on back to the kitchen, fumbling in the darkness beside the door for a switch. The room sprang to light, neatly ordered. She found the marzipan roll in the refrigerator in a plastic bag. One end had been sliced; she could see candied cherries and other fruits.

From the knife rack she took a knife and sliced off a generous piece, then opened cupboard doors until she found a small plate. Sampling a bit of the crumbly, delicious pastry, she decided that what she needed to go with it was a cup of tea.

After opening more cupboard doors, she found some of the familiar Lipton's tea in bags. A cup then while she waited for the kettle to come to a boil on the butane flame. She located a spoon with no difficulty, and started looking through some unmarked canisters for sugar. One held rice and also an ancient key of black iron, about six inches long. Mighty funny place for a key. A hiding place—but hidden from whom? Richard? Did Concepción keep some of her personal belongings locked away? Or had this trusted servant been stealing a few little things? Ah . . . Mimi's clothes. Richard had said he didn't know where she had put them. Obviously, Concepción didn't want her to see them until she'd had a chance to take what she fancied for herself. As if I'd want any of them, Gigi thought.

Back in front of the fireplace in the salon, she sat nibbling contentedly, sipping tea. She was grateful for the small island of warmth. The candle she had lighted on the little table gave just enough of a glow. Outside, the wind blew hard now, and somewhere a shutter was banging, giving eerie emphasis to the wildness of the night.

The silver coffee urn still sat on the table. It was like a mirror in which she saw herself distorted as she finished the last of the pastry and reached for her cup. She stared with glazed, unfocused eyes. If she had been a child again, she could have believed that her image was that of someone else, the curve of the urn making her face strangely elongated, her eyes huge and mysterious. Back of her, she could see the reflection of the room, stretching on to a vastness of space, with tiny furniture that would have been appropriate for the tiny people of that other fantasy of long ago.

Josh Lincoln had said that you can stare at something bright, anything will do, and be hypnotized if you consent to let go of reality.

She stared at the unreality in the silver urn: *And the more times you're hypnotized, the easier it is.*

She might be able to take herself back, all alone, back through the years. Find that long-ago Christmas tree. Find childhood, herself. Find the girl Ann, beautiful and warm and laughing, surrounding her child with the certain, precious knowledge of love.

Gigi stared, willing herself back.

A cold draft moved through the room. A tiny faraway door opened on the tiny faraway balcony. A tiny witch stood there, with a wildness of gray hair. And as Gigi stared, the reflection was broken up with a swift flurry of movement, as when a stone is thrown into a still pond. A door slammed. Her cup rattled into her saucer. Her chair clattered when it fell as she jumped to her feet to whirl about and stare, breathing hard, feeling the warmth of spilled tea seep through her robe.

The warm wetness of the tea was real enough, and so was the pounding of her heart, but how much else had been real? The draft of cold air had surely not been imagined. But the tiny witch on the balcony must have been only a figment of her self-induced trance. It was too frightening to let herself believe otherwise. No one was on the balcony now.

Gigi moved back to stand closer to the fireplace, but the embers gave little warmth and she was very much afraid. The tapestries on the walls shuddered a little in the drafts that swirled in from outside. The blossoms in the big arrangement of Mimi's funeral flowers trembled, dropped some of their petals. The draperies drawn across the windows twitched, as if someone might be standing behind each one of them.

She had the impulse to scream, add her terror to the rising howl of the wind and the insistent banging of that distant shutter. But she was afraid to scream, afraid to attract attention to herself. She blew out the candle and ran, the sound of her own footsteps adding to her fear as she realized they could drown out the sound of stealthy pursuit.

Another thought, more sensible, slowed her steps. What if she had made so much noise with her pounding feet that Richard should appear in the shadows behind her, with puzzled questions that asked her to explain her behavior? How could she tell that reasonable, intelligent man that she had seen a tiny witch?

She reached her door, shut it tight, thankful to be able to turn the key she had been told she would never need. Her room was cold; a window had blown open. She struggled to close it, feeling the cold rain on her face, her hands. She huddled in her bed, trying to warm herself, to calm the fears that she tried to believe must be very foolish.

What I should be most afraid of, she told herself when the thudding of her heart had slowed, is my own mind, my suggestible, impressionable mind. Never again must she run the risk of putting herself in a trance. The tiny witch had surely had no more reality than the tiny girl in the blue dress who stood beckoning, waving her into the golden cottage. She knew the dangers of letting herself believe in any fantasy were as real as the dangers of being drawn into the heart of a fire.

I'm borderline crazy. It was not a cheering thought, but it was better than believing that tonight or at any other time there had ever been a witch in this house.

Once during the night she awoke. The wind whipped at the night, paused, caught breath, and came again with a roar. During the lulls in the wind, a child was crying.

Did she herself, a little girl not yet three, still wander here, crying for her mother? It must be only the moaning cry of the wind. She pulled the covers around her ears so that she could not hear the sound any more.

13

Around ten o'clock the next morning Gigi came downstairs to find Richard playing solitaire at a card table drawn up to the salon windows that overlooked the sea. "Let's go sightseeing."

Richard looked up from his cards with a look of surprise, and then inclined his head toward the windows. "Have you looked out there? Surely you can't be serious."

"Sure. I looked. From my windows I watched the waves crashing while I was eating my breakfast. I think the ocean is exciting in a storm."

"And the roads are half washed out. Anyway, ours will be between here and the village. And you can't see more than fifty meters in any direction."

"Oh, I know. It's not sensible. I didn't mean that I wanted us to get in the car and drive anywhere. But I thought it would be marvelous if we could go for a walk. This place sort of gets to me. I think if I could get out for just an hour or so . . ."

"I'm sorry, Gigi, that things are so dull for you."

"It's not your fault. I'm sorry to be like this. But last night I came downstairs, and . . ."

"I know."

"Did you hear me?"

"No. Concepción mentioned that you had apparently changed your mind about the pastry."

"Was she cross?"

"My dear girl, of course she wasn't cross. We want you to feel at home here."

At home. She could not imagine ever feeling at home here. She said, "Thank you, Richard. And the pastry was just as delicious as you said it would be. But I had an awful scare."

"Did you now." His hand hesitated, holding a red queen before he put it down on a black king. He gave her a humoring smile. "What scared you?"

A tiny witch. Here in the cold gray daylight she could not bring herself to admit anything as crazy. "My own mind, I think. I have a most suggestible mind. I know I sometimes imagine things until they seem to be real. But I do think this house may be haunted."

"Good. I think that we agreed it would be a real drawing card. There is a book around that tells the legends of Ca'n Cornitx. I must look it up and see if we can find anything about a ghost."

"Have you ever seen anything in this house?"

"No. More's the pity. I would love to see a real ghost.

They're solid, you know. Look just like real people. Not the see-through, floaty things that the movies usually provide. D'you know, after our conversation last night, I've given some serious thought to using this house for one of my films. It would be far better than any set we could build. Free too, though I'd charge a pretty penny against expenses."

"Have you ever heard anything?"

"Oh, dear, I am letting you down most dreadfully all around, but I'm afraid a truthful answer will have to be in the negative also. Oh, I've heard noises. It's rather hair-raising at times the way the wind moans along the passages, the way the doors open and close. But there's nothing that's ever happened that couldn't have a natural explanation. As I told you, I incline to the belief that some houses do have ghosts. I've just not been lucky enough to find one here."

She had seated herself across from him. She folded her hands tight on the table. "Last night I heard a child crying."

His smile was indulgent. "Where did it seem to come from?"

"I couldn't tell. I've heard it only when I've been in my room. And with the wind making such a racket, it was hard to place. It seemed to come from outside, and yet . . ."

"We have sea birds that cry."

"At night?"

"Certainly. At night, any time. And the cry—although I've never thought of this before—could sound like a child to a suggestible, imaginative person who sometimes lets her fancy run away with her. Was there anything else?" He scooped his cards together, his eyes on her with anticipation and a glint of amusement he didn't try to hide.

A tiny witch with a halo of wild gray hair.

"Well . . . Richard, I sat here in this room last night,

eating that pastry and drinking a cup of tea that I had made for myself. And there was this icy draft."

"Oh, jolly good. A necessary ingredient of all good ghost stories. And then?"

She didn't answer for a moment. "I have a notion not to go on. You're making such fun of me."

"I apologize. No more jokes."

"And then . . . you see, I was looking at the reflection of the room in the silver coffee urn, and it seemed . . . I thought I saw the door on the right open up there on the balcony. I thought I saw somebody there. And by the time I jumped up and looked around, the door had slammed shut and nobody was there."

"I don't doubt one single word you've said. Wild and stormy as last night was, I am sure that a door did blow open and that Concepción came to close it."

"But it was so late. Nearly midnight. She must have gone to bed by then."

"She has the responsibility of this place. She's the only one in this part of the house, so naturally she knows she must take care of things. After what happened upstairs in December, she is well aware of what damage wind and rain can cause. I'm sure she is alert to the sound of every shutter that bangs."

"Where is her room?"

He gave a wave of his hand. "Out there. Her room opens from a hallway behind the kitchen."

"But"—Gigi summoned her courage—"I saw someone with wild gray hair. Concepción's hair isn't gray."

"It could be. Who knows? Maybe all that hair of hers is just a black wig over wild gray hair."

"You're teasing me again."

His hands covered hers, warm over her cold ones. "Darling Gigi, forgive me. I am very sorry you were frightened last night. Do stay in your room at night after this. Promise?"

"Okay."

"Take some things upstairs to read. That's a detail I forgot, but there wasn't enough time to think of everything. What I most regret, however, is that there is so little diversion for you here. This beastly weather is sure to let up, and then we'll see the whole island. We'll take one day for a drive up to Formentor. And I'll want you to see the caves—the ones at Artá are the largest and quite awe-inspiring."

"I'd like that."

"I'll take you to some of the eating places that, I promise you, are very different from anything you'll find at home. There's a *bodega*, a restaurant in Inca that should be fun for you—vast wine vats, ten times as big as the ones downstairs, and the best suckling pig on the whole island. I'll wager you've never tasted thrush."

"Thrush? Those birds that sing so beautifully? Oh, Richard, I don't think I could ever bring myself to eat one."

"Certainly you could. They net them here on this island. I'll take you to a place where they serve them, a gourmet treat you'll never forget. And Palma—we'll go there and simply raise hell. I'm a member of the Club Nautico and that should be a bit different. I'll see to it that you meet yachtsmen from all over the world. Real international flavor. We've night clubs in Palma, if that's to your taste, quite good theater from time to time, symphony. Do you like ballet?"

"Love it, yes."

"Very well. We can plan. But this afternoon I'm afraid there's not much we can do but stay right here. Do you play chess?"

Gigi was not a chess player. Midafternoon she put on jeans and a comfortable sweater and went downstairs. Nobody was about. It was still raining a little so she went to the kitchen to try to find Concepción and ask if she could borrow again the blue plastic raincoat that she'd worn to Mimi's grave. Concepción was not in the kitchen, but even though the room was quite dark, Gigi saw where the raincoat hung on a hook by the back door.

As she was putting it on, Concepción came from the direction of her room and stared. She turned on the light.

"*Buenas tardes, Concepción.*"

"*Buenas tardes, señorita.*"

The word for borrow, the word for raincoat, escaped Gigi, if she had ever known them. "*Por favor . . .*" She indicated the raincoat.

"*Sí, señorita.*"

Gigi's fingers fumbled with the torn buttonholes. It was the first time today she'd had a chance to study the woman in bright light. It couldn't possibly have been Concepción whom she'd seen last night, even though her size would have been diminished along with everything else in that reflection, and even though she did look a bit like one of the modern self-styled witches who might sneak off to a Sabbat now and then. Her black hair was her own. She might dye it, but the hairline was plainly visible in the dark upward sweep around her face and neck. The coronet of braids on top was a little askew, as if she might have been taking her siesta.

"*La siesta . . . en su cuarto?*" The girl gestured toward the door that led back to Concepción's room.

"*Sí.*"

"*Lo siento*—I am sorry." She smiled.

Concepción gave a small shrug. "*De nada.*" She turned

off the light and walked away. *Why* did she seem so unfriendly? Gigi left by the back door, glad to get out of the
house, glad that Richard had not appeared to try to keep
her from going out in the rain.

The rain was little more than a heavy mist, with fine
droplets, and although the wind had died down, the air was
chilly and she had to walk fast to keep warm. The sea
crashed against the rocky shore, gasped back, rocks rattling
in its throat, then came again, dashing salt spray up into her
face.

She clambered down over the rocks to a narrow strip of
sandy beach, and tried to figure out the best way to get to
the narrow spit that extended out quite a distance, ending in
a tall woman-shaped rock, barely visible through the mist.
Careful not to fall, welcoming the exercise, she jumped
from rock to rock until she reached the spit. It made a
continuous path, although the waves occasionally washed
over the low places.

The Mediterranean, she remembered reading, had little
perceptible rise of the tides, so she did not have to worry
about that. Still, her feet were soon soaked and her wet
hands were numb.

She thought of her bathing suit back there in her suitcase,
wondering if she would have a chance to use it. She wished
for her warm clothes left at home. She remembered that
Spain-bound girl at the airport who had wondered only if
she could get by with a phrase book. Did that poor girl, who
had saved for a year, huddle now miserably in some youth
hostel, waiting for the skies to clear and the sun to start
shining, à la the travel brochures?

Black crablike creatures scrambled on the rocks, staying
out of her way, which was a mercy. The thought of one of
them crawling on her gave her the horrors. Sea birds, gulls

and others she could not identify, plunged from time to time screaming into the sea. Occasionally one would come up with a fish, only to lose it to the viciously curved beak of another bird. Their cries were sharp, ill-tempered, not at all like the sounds she had heard in the night.

When she reached the tall rock at the end of the spit, she saw that if she used her imagination, it still looked a bit like the figure of a giant woman. On the far side of it she found a curving hollow, as if stone skirts had been spread aside to provide a sheltered place from the wind.

What a fine place it would be for sunbathing, Gigi thought as she scrambled up to sit on it. Out of sight of the house, she could strip naked for an all-over tan. If the sun came out—and surely it would sometime while she was on the island—she would put on her bathing suit and come here so as to have some proof of her Majorcan vacation when she got home.

She linked her arms around her wet knees and stared at the leaden sky, the dark, unfriendly sea. She felt a million miles from home, and wished she were there. Her friends at work must be envying her these days on the sunny Mediterranean coast. She should find some post cards showing bathers on bright beaches or diners in cheerful little sidewalk cafés. She would write notes saying, "Wish you were here." And she did, especially Josh Lincoln.

When she got back to her room she would write to him and tell him that Mimi had died. Surely by tomorrow it would be possible to get out and mail a letter.

The solid gray of the clouds had thinned a little. In the western sky a disk appeared. It looked no more like the sun than a circle drawn with a compass on gray paper and painted with thin yellow water color. She could look straight at it.

Far out she could see a ship, quite large, moving slowly, the smoke from its stacks streaming flat and dark behind it. On a clear day it would be fine to sit here with binoculars, moving them about on the horizon. She knew there were other Balearic islands—Ibiza, Minorca, and many little ones which were just rocky dots. She had no idea where any of them were located, but with the aid of binoculars she might be able to spot some of them.

The clouds were thickening again, blotting out the paper sun. The wind must be rising, for she could see huge breakers out in the sea. She was becoming chilly again, just sitting there motionless, but she decided she would wait until that ship on the horizon had steamed out of sight. It was better than going back to that big, gloomy house. Suddenly she realized that keeping her eyes on that distant shape was having an almost hypnotic effect.

She scrambled to her feet. No more trances, thank you. I'm a borderline nut and I know it. So long as I know it . . .

She came out from the protection of the stone skirts, braced herself against the strong wind, and looked with dismay back along the spit that led to the shore. The path disappeared completely from time to time in the angry surge of the waves. Those high breakers she had seen out there must be having their effect.

But the tides here did not rise dangerously. Maybe the full moon made a difference?

The wind caught at the protective raincoat, almost ripping it away from her. Stumbling, slipping, she ran, while the sea birds screamed as if enraged that she had roused in time to get to safety. One of the birds pursued her, diving just past her head and then coming back. Had she disturbed its nest? Her arms over her head, she kept running.

She fell, lay stunned for a moment, the breath knocked

out of her. The water rushed over her, filling her mouth with salt water. She struggled to her feet. Her sneakers, heavy with sand, slowed her as if she ran in a nightmare, slow-motion. She had lost the rocky spit—it had just disappeared. In water up to her knees, with sliding sand being sucked beneath her, she screamed for help, knowing she sounded like the birds and that her puny imitation was instantly dispersed by the wind.

Blinded by salt water, the wind whipping her hair into her eyes, she could not even see the narrow strip of beach where she had started out. She fell again and a wave sucked her back. She turned over and over. She could swim, but not against this.

She swam against it. Or perhaps her feeble flailing had nothing to do with her being washed up on the shore, left momentarily while the sea receded to gather strength that would enable it to come at her again, capture her, keep her for its own.

Not quite. Not yet. Choking on salt water, she reached for an outthrust rock, held on, reached again. Her hand encountered something. A root. She tugged herself up, free of the waves that would have devoured her.

A huge rock came hurtling, bouncing, barely missing her. She must have dislodged it by tugging at the tree root. But the jagged rocks under her hands now were firm. Rocks like these had killed her mother, but now their firm handholds were saving her life.

A hand reached down, warm, soft as a woman's. Gigi clung, felt herself being drawn upward. Through drowned eyes that had looked at death, she saw Richard's face and was surprised. For frantic moments she had been so sure that no human help would save her that she had almost, at first touch, believed the reaching hand was not of this world, a possible miracle here on this island where people, like children, still believed.

He said, quite calm, "Why did you go out there?"

"I thought . . . I didn't know there were tides here."

"Nonsense. This time of year when the moon is full we can sometimes get a foot or more. And when there's a wind whipping the waves, or a ground swell—My God, when I saw you there in that last bit of water!"

Gigi wished he wouldn't sound as if he were lecturing her. She looked down at herself, wondering where the raincoat had gone. Her nails were broken. One wrist throbbed as if she had sprained it.

Richard took off his coat and put it around her. "You're cold as a fish. Come on, do you think you can make it to the house? I'm not at all sure I could carry you, but Concepción—"

"No, not Concepción!"

He said in a mild reproof, "It was she who alerted me. She came to my room, alarmed when you did not come back. I got out my binoculars and saw you coming along that spit. I knew it wasn't terribly deep there yet, but I could see the breakers coming in, and if you had fallen and struck your head, it could have been quite a nasty business. I got there just in time to give you a hand up. Not that you weren't managing perfectly well enough by then. I say, you've got rather a nasty scratch on your face. It's bleeding a bit."

"Salt water is a good antiseptic." She was not going to have him think that a narrow escape from death could keep her from having a stiff upper lip. Pip, pip, and all that.

"My dear—" His cane was in one hand and he steadied her with the other as he gave her his grave, sweet smile. "I really am tremendously relieved that you're all right. A cold dip never hurt anyone—I'm just enough of a Britisher to believe that—but right now you're trembling and your lips are blue and I think you must hurry into a hot tub."

"All right." Her teeth were chattering with nerves and chill.

"I've already sent Concepción up to get a fire going in your room and light the Butano in the bath. I think I'll also have her take a mug of hot buttered rum up to you. Mimi is—*was*—always a great believer in that. You're to drink it all. And then get into your bed for a bit of a snooze before dinner."

Gigi did exactly as she was told. When she woke up, it was morning.

14

A note lay on the breakfast tray outside Gigi's room. Still feeling sodden from her round-the-clock sleep, she unfolded the single sheet. And then gave a little cry. For two whole days she was to be left alone in this house!

She slumped in a chair by the window. Dull light from another rainy sky fell on the sheet of notepaper in her hand. Richard had written with obvious haste: "A chap just came up with a message. I am needed on the peninsula, so I'm rushing to catch the early plane. A great nuisance for me, and I'm sure a disappointment for you to be left at loose ends for two days, but I promise to make it up to you when I come back. Cheerio, then, until Saturday."

"I could *bawl!*" She wadded the note and hurled it at the fireplace.

She ate breakfast, peeled an orange, drank the coffee, which by now was tepid. Her sleep, which she had badly needed to catch up on, had refreshed her, but the renewal of energy made her feel like a wild creature trapped in a cage.

If only he had wakened her to take her with him! She could have stayed in Palma, could even have gone with him as far as Barcelona or Madrid, or wherever the plane had taken him. Two days of sightseeing in the rain would have been much better than this. It would have been lovely to have prowled the museums, shopped, talked to people. In the cities she was sure they at least made an attempt at English.

When she got up she was conscious of muscular soreness from yesterday's bout with the elements. Two days! She had to fill them in somehow.

She sat at the desk, blew off the pollen that had fallen from the little round mimosa blossoms, and started a letter to Josh. She told him first of Mimi's death and how hard it was to believe that bubbly, happy little person had vanished from her life. Then she told him about Richard—she liked him—and about Concepción—she didn't like her.

Thoughtfully, she nibbled the end of her pen. If she chose, quite a dramatic story could be made out of yesterday afternoon's adventure. It was scary even now to remember the savage might of the waves that had tossed her like a leaf as she fought for breath, for a footing on the sucking sand. That great boulder that had come crashing down could very easily have killed her. But to tell Josh all that would only confirm his belief that she wasn't quite able to take care of herself.

"Yesterday I went swimming. Accidentally, that is. You must have seen post cards of the sun-kissed beaches and the blue Mediterranean—I'll try to find one to send you. That sea may be blue sometimes, but yesterday it wasn't and I was . . ."

It took a whole page to describe the house. She promised to take pictures if the sun ever came out.

"Love, Gigi." She looked at the signature, which she had written automatically. Over the years she must have signed a thousand letters that way. It didn't have to mean anything. Josh would know that. But maybe . . .

Careful. Right now, feeling lonely and a little bit lost, was no time to make up her mind that she loved Josh Lincoln.

When she had sealed the letter, she thought she might walk to Son Baraitx to mail it, but she changed her mind when she stepped out onto the balcony. The air was heavy. The leaden sky looked as if it could let go with more rain at any moment.

On the left, the muddy, potholed road led down the hill in the direction of the village. On the right, the stone walls of the house straggled upward. She saw now where the raw boards had been nailed over some of the upper windows. No doubt the whole place could be lovely again when it was repaired, when the sloping gardens were restored, and when the rich guests that Richard envisioned thronged the terraces in bright dresses. But right now it was bleak, and in her mind would always be the thought, if not the memory, of her mother's body on the rocks below. Oh, she could not wait to get away from here!

Careful of the scratch on her cheek, Gigi washed her face, then dressed, groaning a little as she raised her arms to pull on a white turtleneck sweater. What she needed was exercise to limber up her sore muscles. A swim. Sure, sure. A walk. Even that had been denied her by this miserable weather.

Why couldn't Richard have wakened her before he left? He couldn't have been in that much of a hurry. He knew how she felt about Concepción. *Men.* Honestly. Even Josh Lincoln sometimes treated her like a child. What was it he called her sometimes? Dum-dum. Very funny. She knew she was being unreasonable and she didn't care.

She carried her tray down to the kitchen and exchanged unsmiling greetings with Concepción. She supposed she ought to look in her phrase book and see if she could figure out a way to tell her she was sorry she had lost that ugly raincoat and would buy her another.

Concepción had put a stack of records on the hi-fi, which played doleful music so irritatingly loud that it could have been piped through loudspeakers for a state funeral. Gigi turned it off, and immediately Concepción turned on the radio in the kitchen, equally loud. A war of nerves? The woman was deaf?

The morning dragged horridly. Gigi played solitaire for a while, then remembered the television set she had seen in the music room. She found it after opening only a couple of wrong doors. The set was old, black-and-white, with a waning picture tube. For a while she amused herself rather drearily by watching a Lucille Ball episode which, judging by hair styles and clothes, must be nearly twenty years old. Spanish words emerged from the mouths of Lucy and the others. Some of it was pretty fakey, but she supposed it was remarkable that they could do it at all.

Concepción passed by the door and looked in a couple of times. Gigi wondered if Richard had told the woman to watch her and make sure she didn't do anything foolish, like trying to get into that room up there where the roof had fallen in.

He needn't have worried, she thought crossly. She had no wish to get her head bashed in, nor the slightest desire to do further exploring. This house was not hers. She didn't belong here. And as for Richard's suggestion that she could have any of the objects that caught her fancy, she didn't feel that she had any more right to them than to the pieces on display in a museum.

But she did want a good book to read. In the library, she looked through the shelves, hoping to find the book Richard had mentioned that told about Ca'n Cornitx. *Ca'n Cornitx: Las Legendas.* She pulled it down. It was, of course, in Spanish.

At least half the books were in Spanish; they looked as if they had been bought with the house, and most of them were old. This unaired, cavernous room with its dank smell of rotting leather, dust, and mice, would make—she was sorry she'd had the thought—a good hiding place for a snake. Quickly, she selected a couple of the newer-looking books, hoping one of them would help her through the hours ahead.

As she left the library she remembered all the bright-jacketed books she had seen in Richard's room. He wouldn't mind if she had a look through them, she was sure. But the door was locked. Gigi looked around her, wondering if she had made a mistake. No, this had to be his room, next to the gruesome painting of the man with his head cut off. She tucked the books under her arm and used both hands on the knob, thinking it might only be difficult to open.

Concepción's loud voice startled her. She was coming quickly toward her.

"I just wanted a book—*un libro*—" Gigi knew her words might not make much sense since she already had two books. "*Un otro libro.*"

"*No, señorita, no, no!*" She was pointing at what looked like a small Yale lock that Gigi had not noticed before, and saying something about a key. "*Esto es el cuarto del señor Ricardo!*"

"I know that. I just wanted . . ." Concepción's manner could not have been more accusing if she had found her trying to break into that safe in there. Oh, what was the use! Gigi gave an exclamation of annoyance, feeling color rise in her cheeks as she walked from the corridor into the salon.

What was the *matter* with that woman? Had the delegation of a bit of authority gone to her head? As Gigi tossed the books onto a table, she was struck by a sudden thought. Did Concepción think that she was trying to find Mimi's clothes? That could very well be the answer and it did make a little sense. The poor thing could have every last stitch, every pelt, every feather, every rhinestone. The two of them might get on a little better if she could just put Concepción's mind to rest on that score.

What was the word for clothes? *Ropas.* Gigi looked around as Concepción was about to go through the door that led to the kitchen. "Concepción, *las ropas de la señora* . . . I do not want. *Yo no quiero* . . . no, no *nada, nada.*" Gigi shook her head and made gestures of rejection with her hands. "No, no, *nada, nada.*"

Concepción only stared at her blankly, as if she didn't have the slightest idea what the girl was talking about. She inclined her head with servile hostility. "*Sí, señorita.*"

Baffled, Gigi went to stand at the window, staring out at the gray rain, the gray sea, the gray sky. Of course, most of

Mimi's things would be too small for Concepción, but still, the furs were valuable, and would probably enhance Concepción's image of herself as a movie star. Well, it was no concern of hers. Why couldn't she just laugh it off?

No. In this house I do not feel like laughing or pretending that anything is the least bit amusing. I hate this house and it hates me back. And if it is trying to tell me something, I do not want to hear. I just want to close my ears to the strange noises. I just want to close my eyes, not look at any more pictures with their bright, warm-looking blood, not risk glimpsing anything more that will frighten me. I don't want to know what goes on in Concepción's mind. Out there in the kitchen now she is pretending to get lunch —all right, she is getting lunch—but from time to time I know she takes little peeks at me. That door has creaked open and shut a couple of times.

Or was it that door on the right up there on the balcony that had creaked open and shut? Had some dreadful little witchlike thing come to stare at her?

Gigi whirled around and looked up. Nobody was on the balcony. She wished she could completely convince herself that nobody had been there the other night, that her mind had just played a schizophrenic trick. If she had a choice, which would she choose—a mind that made wildly inappropriate responses to quite ordinary things, or a little old witch? *Miss Lang, what will you have? I think I'll have just one sunshiny day, Doctor. Never mind about the shock therapy, just one sunshiny day and a fast goodbye.*

Lunch. It was meager, but Gigi was not hungry. The fire now in the big cavernous fireplace was meager too, as if Concepción had her own sweet way about things when the master was away.

Concepción came to clear the little table. "*La siesta*

ahora, señorita." She said it firmly, almost like a command. *"Sí, sí, la siesta ahora."*

Gigi had no wish for a siesta now, nor did she have any wish to remain in front of this stingy fire any longer. She got up dutifully and went back along the corridor. Up in her own room, she would make a fine, big, extravagant fire. She would, if it pleased her, turn on the Butano wastefully in the bathroom.

But when she opened her door she saw that the room was pale with thin sunlight. She dashed out to the balcony and looked up at the sky. The clouds were breaking up. She could even see bits of scattered blue. It must not be going to rain any more. Let Concepción have her siesta, she knew what she was going to do!

15

Gigi pulled on a denim jacket, hurried down the stairs, through the courtyard, giving no thought to the snake or to anything else but the glorious prospect of getting out of that gloomy house for a while. Already some of the notions she'd had were beginning to diminish.

Rain had made the narrow road much worse than when she and Richard had driven up it that first night. At one place she could see where the tire marks of his little car had detoured to avoid a washout. She jumped over the ruts, not quite as nimbly as she might have done if her leg muscles hadn't been so stiff, but she knew the exercise would be good for her.

From time to time the sun disappeared completely, but

visibility was good and the landscape that opened before her had a strange, lonely loveliness. Everything was so still. She heard only the sound of her own feet and the distant crashing of the sea on the rocks below.

On the other side of her, the mountains lifted; their tops were lost in low-hanging clouds, but she was able to count six terraces whose stone walls held back the ancient olive trees. One of the trees seemed to emerge from a cave, to be poised, ready to spring and catch something in its crippled arms. Not her. She had escaped the house and Concepción's dark watching eyes, and when she got back she felt that she would be able to endure the rest of her days there—not many—with better grace after an afternoon of freedom.

She would go home early next week, she decided. She didn't want to hurt Richard's feelings, but what possible reason could there be for her to stay longer?

Clean cold water poured from a viaduct on the mountain, and fresh green grass had sprung up at the edge of the overflow. At the side of the road little plants were thrusting new leaves. Gigi stooped to peer closely; some of them looked exactly like the jack-in-the-pulpits that she had known back in Illinois. She went on, cheered by the link with the familiar. Home, she reminded herself, was only a few hours away. She had only to decide to go, and then go.

Not that she had a home the way Josh did. Home for him was that farm in Ohio. She wondered if before long she would find herself walking with him over those acres that he loved. Would she be tempted to lie, say "I do" just because of this hunger for roots, her own place? Maybe smart girls lied. And then hoped and tried. But she did not have to make up her mind today about Josh Lincoln.

A tinkling bell. Sheep. They were surprised by her as she came around a curve, and ran foolishly as if they thought she might climb over the stone wall to harm them. Watching the sheep, she noticed a little stone house. No, not really a house, it seemed to be little more than the front wall of a house built into the side of the mountain, with one window, a chimney, and a door. Who would live in a place like that—a shepherd, or someone who gathered sticks to sell in the village? Perhaps even a poet might live there, some fugitive from civilization who contented himself with a snug fire on cold nights and that splendid view of the sea. She was tempted to climb up there. Her ready imagination provided her with a cozy scene where she ate cheese and bread and wine, imbibing, with the wine, words of wisdom from someone who felt the world well lost. Once, as short a time as a year ago, she remembered that she had wished for solitude, but that time had passed. Today, especially, she felt the need for companionship. She hoped she would meet someone in the village to talk to. Definitely, she was going to try to find Catalina.

Another curve. And there, spread suddenly before her, was the village of Son Baraitx, the cross-topped steeple of its church lifting golden in the pale sun. She wished that she had remembered to bring her camera. Words could never do justice to the look of that town from here. Roofs of different heights, tiled with pale gradations of sienna, seemed to top houses that were built together, their walls curving down, out, and up from the hub of the church. Cypress trees were like dark-green exclamation points thrusting upward to the sky. There were palm trees, too, at this lower altitude, and again the softening loveliness of almond blossoms, their fragrance, haunting and sweet, wafting toward her.

She hurried, the wind blowing her hair. She had seen no one, but as she neared the main road, a brightly painted high-wheeled cart, drawn by one horse, came clopping smartly down the street from the village. A ruddy-cheeked driver in white shirt and suspenders touched his black hat to her in friendly fashion and turned where the road sign pointed to Sóller.

Now Gigi could hear loud voices and laughter. It sounded for all the world like a party. As she rounded the corner to take the road that led up to the village, she saw an open structure on her right where several women were washing their clothes in long stone troughs. Water poured in a constant stream from a pipe that extended from the side of the mountain. Sleeves, rolled up, revealed muscular arms, bright red from the cold water. For just a moment the women gave her covert glances and were silent, then they resumed their shouting conversation. Gigi wondered if they washed their clothes while their husbands took their siesta, or if the promise of clearing weather had brought them here now.

At the left, a café. Chairs on the terrace leaned toward the tables, telling her that the time for tourists was not yet. Too bad. It would have been fun to have stopped there, struck up a conversation with somebody, almost anybody, who spoke her language.

The street curved upward steeply now. *Correo.* That meant post office. Gigi walked up the steps and through an open door into a dark, cold room. No one was there. "Hello —*hola?*" Apparently the place was closed until mail time, but if she could buy just one stamp to mail Josh's letter . . . She raised her voice, "*Señor—por favor?*"

A door opened at the back and a woman stood there. She wore many layers of clothing, topped by a heavy jacket. "*Cerrado . . . cerrado,*" she said loudly. A black-eyed child came to cling to her skirts, looking around shyly.

"*Sí, cerrado.* I know it's closed, but—" Gigi held up the letter, pointing to the place for the stamp.

The woman was shaking her head. "*Lo siento—lo siento.*" Some rapid words then that seemed to mean that her husband was the one who sold the stamps. "*A las cinco.*" She held up five fingers and gestured toward the clock on the dark wall. It was now only a quarter of three.

"*Dónde está—*" Gigi hesitated, trying to remember the word for store. It was stupid of her not to have brought her little book. "*La tienda. Dónde está la tienda?*"

A look of astonishment. For a moment Gigi thought she must have used the wrong word, perhaps one that was highly improper, but then the woman picked up the child and came hurrying past Gigi to the door. She pointed. "*La tienda . . . la tienda! Allí . . . allí!*" She said the words as if she could not believe that everyone in the world would not know where the store was.

Gigi thanked her and saw the store in plain enough sight when she started up the hill again. It was on the central square, from which the streets and flights of steps spiraled outward like the arms of an octopus. The church, imposing from here, loomed high above what seemed to be the town well, where an old woman in black was filling a bright-red plastic bucket.

A large display of straw shopping baskets sat in front of the store. Gigi went past them to read the sign on the door that said the place was closed between one and three. She cupped her hands to look inside. It was dark; no one was there, but she heard steps descending almost as if the approach of a customer might have been noted from living quarters above. A girl appeared at the back, turned on a light, and came to unlock the door.

"Buenas tardes." She was young, with a pleasant smile. *"Buenas tardes."*

The girl gave a wave to her hand, inviting Gigi to come inside and take a look around.

"Momentito." Gigi touched the girl's arm. *"Habla usted inglés?"*

"No, señorita." There followed a fast spiel about her sister who could *"habla inglés muy bien"* but the sister was sick or away or busy or something. Gigi knew only that the words added up to the fact that she was going to have to make do with a few Spanish words and a lot of sign language.

"Dónde está Catalina? Necesito encontra Catalina . . ."

The girl laughed, shaking her head and starting to count on her fingers. *"Catalina . . . Catalina . . . Catalina . . . cuál Catalina?"*

There were many Catalinas, as Richard had said. How to say it? Gigi held up the fingers of both hands twice and then lifted two more. *"Veinte y dos años—Catalina en los Estados Unidos."*

"Ah, sí, sí." The girl's face cleared. *"La hermana de padre—tía Catalina. Ella vive en Sevilla."* She said some more words, her hand reaching high to indicate a tall husband, then down as if patting the heads of many children.

Gigi was disappointed, but not surprised to learn that Catalina, apparently the girl's aunt, no longer lived here. She tried to explain that Catalina had taken care of her many years ago, but she was not sure the girl understood although she was nodding and smiling politely while she turned on more lights so Gigi could look around the store.

A bewildering assortment of merchandise was jammed, piled, crowded, stacked to the ceiling: canned goods, cosmetics, medicines, candy, shoes, stationery, cigars, cigarettes, clothing, wines, comic books. A large display of Campbell's soup was on a shelf next to unwrapped bread, some of it in loaves two feet long, others flat and round and big as dishpans. Vegetables, not all of them familiar to Gigi, were spilling out of bins, and some of them, knobby and rootlike, were heaped on the floor. She stepped over them and paused before a case that held several different kinds of cheese. She wished she knew the name of the goat's-milk cheese Josh had said he liked. She might be able to stop by here the day she left and take him some.

One long counter held gifts. Mantillas in rayon lace, gaudy Spanish shawls, plastic ashtrays in the shape of the island, plastic crucifixes, Madonnas with garishly painted faces, drinking mugs that said *Salud!* It was no surprise to see that many of the items had Japan stamped on the back.

She found a small bowl of olive wood for Max and Carol, and a cute little straw burro for their little girl, which Carol, careful mother, could hang as a decoration if she was afraid to let Malinda touch it. Josh, she hoped, would like a dark sculpture of a caballero to sit on his desk.

At the counter beside the cash register, she picked up a paperback that had bright illustrations of Majorcan trees and flowers. On impulse, she decided to buy it for Josh's mother. She bought post cards, discovered that the girl also had stamps for sale, paid with a Spanish bill she'd exchanged dollars for in Washington, and received a bewildering number of pesetas which she didn't bother to count, having no idea of their value.

As she affixed the stamp to Josh's letter, Gigi thought about all the days it would take to reach him, and then she remembered that Richard had said he came here to use the telephone. Why not call Josh right now? At home it was midmorning. He would be at work.

She wrote down the number, and without too much difficulty got the idea across that she wanted the girl to place a long-distance call, and that she would pay for it if the girl would get the charges from the operator.

The phone was beside the stairway at the back of the store. Gigi sat on the stairs and in no time at all Josh Lincoln's voice was on the line, magically coming across the miles to wrap itself about her with love and concern.

"Oh, Gigi, I am so sorry she is dead. It must have been pretty bad to be greeted with such news. But I should have thought the funeral could have waited until you got there."

"No. According to Spanish law, the funeral has to be held within twenty-four hours. That part was all right, Josh. I'm not very good about funerals."

"I'm going to come. I can get a pass and be there by this time tomorrow."

She was tempted, but she said, "Josh, it doesn't make sense. I'd rather you didn't."

"Gigi, I really think I should come. I'll call you tonight."

"You can't. The phone is out of order. I'm calling now from a store in the village. Look, I'll be back in Washington before you know it. Our planes might pass each other in the air."

"When do you think you'll be back?"

"Early next week. I might even leave before then."

"Are you sure you're okay? Your voice doesn't sound quite right."

"I'm okay. Really. The whole thing has been kind of . . . you know . . ."

"What do you think of what's-his-name?"

"Oh, Richard is darling. He's handsome, talented, brilliant, sweet."

"Spare me the adjectives. I don't like the idea of your being there alone with him if he's all that great."

She laughed. "I'm perfectly safe."

"I love you, Gee."

She said softly, "I'm trying to keep this call to three minutes. Hey, one thing—I bought a book for your mother. I thought we could take it to her when we go."

"Does that mean . . . ?"

A wasteful pause. "Josh, I feel just the same. You're my best friend."

A sound from him that would have been hard to spell. "Okay, friend. But you say the word and I'll be there."

"We'll talk about it when I get back. The word right now is stay—"

The operator interrupted to say that their three minutes were up. Feeling good, Gigi hung up. It took most of the pesetas she had received in change to pay for the call, but it had been worth it. More customers were coming into the store now. Smiling at everybody, knowing some of them must have attended Mimi's funeral, Gigi went out onto the square.

While she was in the store the clock in the bell tower had struck three, so she had time to wander a bit before she went back to Ca'n Cornitx. She hoped she would meet somebody she could really talk to.

A taxi had drawn up before a long flight of steps that led upward. An elderly woman got out, her white hair style similar to Gigi's, her all-weather coat a bright pink. She was loaded with what looked like a heavy market basket and a small overnight case. She exchanged rapid Spanish with the driver when she paid him.

Gigi was disappointed. She had thought the woman

looked like someone with whom she might speak her own language.

The clock in the steeple struck three again. Gigi had started to walk away, but now she paused and looked up at it, perplexed.

"Oh, it does that," the woman said.

Gigi looked at her, delighted. "How did you know that I . . . ?"

"Oh, I can always tell. You're an American, aren't you?"

"Yes. I'm Virginia Lang. Just doing the touristy bit, looking around."

"And I'm Octavia Milton." She put down her things and reached to give Gigi a firm handshake. Her lipstick matched the young, bright pink of her coat. "Every stranger wonders about our clock. It strikes twice in case someone might not have heard it the first time—or so it was explained to me when I first came here to live many years ago. I imagine the town fathers decided on that at a time when not many people had timepieces." She leaned to pick up her market basket and suitcase.

"Could I help you carry . . . ?"

"Oh, I can manage perfectly well." She smiled at Gigi, her warm brown eyes twinkling. "I think you may withdraw your offer when I tell you that there are a hundred and seventy-four steps to my house."

"Wow!" Gigi gave a shake to her blond head. "You must live on top of the whole village. Oh, please, I was going to walk around the town and I would love to see it from up there. I'll not mind the steps at all."

Gigi found that she did mind the steps; they were bumpy, cobblestoned, differing in width and height, but this elderly woman was taking them easily, chattering non-stop as she explained that she had been in Palma for a week.

"My annual treat. I see my doctor, get my hair done, go to the symphony. It's lovely, but I am always so glad to get back."

A burro, loaded with bundles of sticks, came clattering up the steps behind them. Gigi's new friend exchanged greetings with the driver, as she did with everyone they saw. Old women, two or three at least, in long black dresses, sat crocheting in the pale sun, the doors behind them opening into very similar neat, dark interiors where Gigi could glimpse beehive fireplaces with no fires, shelves with rows of plates and mugs, tiles on the walls catching glints of light from outside. Many of the houses seemed to have just one room to each floor, with stairs going upward. The finer houses had courtyards that could be seen through grilled gates. All were bright with flowers and orange and lemon trees.

Gigi paused, her excuse being that she wanted to admire the view.

"Do come along. The view is much better from my house. In a minute you'll be able to see it. We're more than halfway there."

She trotted briskly ahead, her legs muscular and her feet firm in their crepe-soled shoes. Gigi had a hard time keeping up with her. She said breathlessly, "You really don't mind the steps, do you, Mrs. Milton?"

"Please call me Octavia. It makes me feel young. No, I love the steps. If it hadn't been for them, I'm sure arthritis or something would have me in a wheelchair by now. I'm seventy-four. My doctor tells me that climbing is very good for my arteries, my heart, my lungs. Did you know that people who live in mountainous regions live the longest?"

Gigi had barely enough breath to say no.

"But more important, the steps give me the privacy I

must have for my work. I'm trying to finish my husband's book. Now that I've had my holiday, I'll plunge right in and finish it. I'll not answer the door— Oh, I become a dreadful person when I'm working, but my friends understand that I must do justice to the project he started. Victor was an archaeologist. He came here to study the prehistoric ruins. We found this place and fell in love with it many years ago. We retired here. Victor is gone now and I'm sometimes lonely, but I have to resist getting involved with the bridge playing and the cocktail partying of the little English-speaking group here. I don't even have a telephone, which they find hard to understand. Lovely people. Perhaps you have met some of them?"

"No. I've been here such a short time."

"Where are you staying?"

"At Ca'n Cornitx. It's up the—"

Octavia Milton stopped, set down her suitcase, and reached her hands toward Gigi. "Ca'n Cornitx! Oh, my dear child, you must be Gigi!"

"Yes, yes, I am."

"Mimi has told me about you. You're the granddaughter she goes to visit! Tell me, how is she? I've not been in touch recently, but I know she's been very ill."

"She . . ." Gigi looked away and then back into the warm brown eyes. "She died."

"Oh, no! Oh, I am sorry, so sorry, to hear that. When did she die?"

"I'm all mixed up on days. She died the day before I came. She was buried the day I got here—that was three days ago. It seems so much longer."

"What a pity that you didn't get to see her before she died. She would have loved seeing you."

172

"Yes, I know. I came at once when I got the cable that she was so ill."

Octavia Milton was shaking her head sadly. "Every time I go away it seems that something bad happens. Antonio, the taxi driver, was telling me that Carlos, the dear old man who helps me garden, died while I was gone. Oh, this must be so dreadful for you. And for Richard. Poor man, he was so devoted to her, so good to her these last months while she's been so sick. I went there to call, shortly before Christmas. Mimi was wretchedly thin, but so cheerful, so effervescent, insisting that she had just torn a ligament or wrenched her back or something that no one need worry about at all."

"Yes. She wanted everybody to be happy. Life was a party."

"And we did go to some marvelous parties in that house, my husband and I. Of course, she was never an intimate friend, but she came to see me when Victor died, almost a year ago. She seemed to sense that she couldn't cheer me up about losing him, so she talked about you during most of our visit. Oh, Gigi, I'm so glad we met. Come now, we must hurry on up and I'll make you a cup of tea."

They rounded a stone wall, smothered under a vine that burst with little star-shaped flowers, and Octavia Milton pointed upward. A house of ancient stone sat at the top of the last flight of steps. The yellow shutters were exactly the same hue as the fruit on the heavily burdened lemon trees. The gate that opened into the courtyard was painted to match.

"*Mi casa es su casa*— You know a little Spanish, don't you? Do feel free to wander anywhere you like, Gigi, while I make us some tea."

She wandered. The house appeared to be almost as old as Ca'n Cornitx, but it was intimate, totally charming, with cozy rooms and steps leading unexpectedly to different levels. Water colors hung on the walls, depicting local scenes. They may not have been of museum quality, but they were a relief after the heavy oils depicting dismembered corpses. Pastel chintzes brought the brightness of fruit and flowers in from the terrace.

Gigi stood leaning her hands on the low wall, awed by the splendor of the view over the rooftops of Son Baraitx. There was a river she had not seen. There were roads that she would like to explore, losing themselves in the soft gray distance. The clouds had thickened again, but a momentary shaft of light, almost like a searchlight, seemed to turn on and pierce the grayness to show her another village some distance away, nestling in the valley. This must be one of the most beautiful places in the world, she thought. Oh, I don't hate Majorca!

Tea, then. They sat on the terrace to sip it and eat the almond cakes which Octavia said she had taken from her freezer.

"A freezer—ah, yes, it's so marvelous having it. When we first came here we didn't even have electricity. Nor a real bathroom, just a dear little place in the garden. I always had masses of flowers planted in front of it. One could sit there and look through the flowers down over the town and up to the mountains. Absolutely sweet. A friend from the States sat in there all of one morning and painted a water color that won her a prize when she got home. One could see the dark, splintery uprights on either side of the partly opened door, and in the foreground the morning light shining through the white irises. She called it 'Toilet in the Garden.' Can't you imagine many viewers being puzzled by that title?" She gave a little giggle, unexpectedly girlish.

Gigi threw back her head and burst into a high laugh of her own. She realized that this was the first time in many days that she had sounded like her old self. "You're trying to cheer me up—and doing it. You wouldn't believe the way I've been moping around that house up there. I don't really like Ca'n Cornitx."

"I'd hardly expect you to, with Mimi gone."

"That's part of it—most of it. The weather's not been any help, and I don't like Concepción."

"Poor Concepción. Don't be too hard on her. She's really a misfit in this town, puts on airs, you know, spoiled by all the years at Ca'n Cornitx. She's one of a family of several girls, the best-looking one, but she's never married and I think she is the main support of her parents. The girls are all good workers—her sister works for me on Mondays—but not overburdened with brains. Concepción may have a little more sense than the others, but she's not really very bright."

"She can't be. Any grown woman who would make a pet of a snake. I know kids do sometimes, but—"

"A snake? Surely it's not in the house."

"Yes, it is. Richard said so. He seemed pretty calm about it. He said it keeps down the rats and mice. But the whole idea seems sick. It gives me the creeps."

"I think the islanders don't have quite the feeling about snakes that we do. You see, there are no poisonous snakes on Majorca—just little garter snakes and then the bigger ones that look like our black snakes at home. I've seen them a few times in the rock walls of my garden. I'll confess I'd just as soon they'd go somewhere else, but Carlos—oh, poor Carlos!—says they eat the garden pests."

It was so good to have somebody to talk to. Gigi looked at the calm face of her new friend. Her skin had the look of taffeta, thin, delicate, as if it had been crumpled many times and then smoothed out with fair success except for the crinkles around the young-looking brown eyes. Gigi said, "It's not the snake itself that bothers me so much—I don't think I have quite the fear of them that some people do. It's just that it sort of seems to fit Concepción's personality. She's cold, unfriendly. She watches me. She makes me think that she suspects me of being about to steal something."

"Well, I know that must be upsetting, but let me say one more thing in defense of Concepción. After several years servants sometimes get so they think they own the place. I've seen that happen more than once. Now that Mimi is gone, she must know that it may not be her home much longer. I expect she's worried as to what is going to become of her."

"Richard has promised her a part in a film."

"You can't be serious! Oh, come now. Concepción doesn't have sense enough to learn lines, and I'm sure she can't act."

"Richard says that doesn't matter."

"Oh." She lifted slim shoulders in a little shrug and passed the cakes again. "I know nothing whatever about the way films are made, and I know Richard knows a great deal. Perhaps he'll be able to get back to all that now. I'm sure he can't have been able to spend much time on his business these last few months."

"He's over there now."

"So soon?"

"Yes. He left this morning and won't be back until Saturday. Something came up that demanded his attention. He left me a note."

176

"I'm surprised that he'd leave with you there, but then, maybe it's sensible for him to plunge right into his work. He's very smart, very talented, and everyone on the island seems to regard him highly. As the saying goes, he knows everybody who is anybody. Now I suppose we shall be losing him. Will you sell the house?"

Gigi's silver-blue eyes widened. She blinked a couple of times.

"Oh, forgive me. It's none of my business. And anyway, it's probably much too soon for you to have made a decision."

"Octavia, the decision is not mine to make. The house is not mine to sell."

"But I thought . . ." Octavia Milton set her teacup down. "Oh, my dear, Mimi herself told me that the place would be yours. Have you talked to the lawyer?"

"No, just to Richard. He explained things to me. Oh, I don't *like* that house. I don't want that house. I'm glad I don't have to own it!"

"But you could sell it. I'm sure Mimi wouldn't want you to feel any responsibility whatever to keep it if you don't like it. It must be worth quite a lot."

"I don't think it's worth much. It's in such a bad state of repair. The top floor of the main part of the house fell in when they had the bad December storms. Anyhow, there's no use thinking about it. Richard loves it and I want him to have it. He has all sorts of great plans for fixing it up, turning it into a sort of *parador*."

"Oh. Then that's that. Mimi could have changed her mind there at the last. Do have another of the almond cakes. Concepción's sister brings the almonds to me every fall at harvest time and I grind them for these cakes. There's nothing in them but honey and almonds and eggs. Fattening, of course, but you don't look as if you had to worry about that. I'll give you a little packet of them when you leave. But first, I want to show you some of the artifacts my husband dug up. Many of them were found near Artá and they'll go to the museum there eventually, but I like having them near me while I'm working on the book. Sometimes it seems almost as if they tell me things—or is that too far out for you to accept? I can't have you thinking that living by myself has turned me into a dotty old woman."

"Not dotty. And you'll never be old." Gigi gave a squeeze to her arm as they went into the house.

A long shelf over the desk in the study held small pieces of ancient pottery, some of them like dolls, one a bull's head carved of reddish stone, and various articles of adornment, beads and rings. Gigi took a shard of pottery into her hands, her fingers moving over it. "A person with the gift of—what is that word?—psychometry could hold this, I suppose, and see back into time."

"Can you?"

"Heavens, no. I was hypnotized a couple of times and then I seemed to go back. But I don't know how safe it is to mess around with all that."

"Nor do I. I half believe in some of it. A woman once visited us here and she claimed she could psychometrize. She held a fragment of pottery much like the one you are holding now and said it had been part of a vessel that held oil. She said she could hear a woman weeping, and that the oil had been used to anoint a dead child."

Gigi put the piece back on the shelf quickly. "I don't want to hear things, to see things that aren't real."

"My husband was like that. He was a practical man, a real scientist. He arrived at his conclusions by making careful measurements, exhaustive studies of the site before he'd allow the first shovel to be put into the ground. And then he'd end up on his knees with tiny brushes and digging tools that looked as if they belonged to a dentist. His special interest was the talayots."

"The . . . ?"

"Talayots. Those are the prehistoric stone structures one sees in so many places about the island. They date back to about fifteen hundred years before Christ. The earlier ones were cone-shaped, and the later ones were square, more like pyramids. Some may have been used only as burial monuments, but others seem to have been fortified dwellings, with rooms built around central pillars. Tunnels have been found, and remains of outbuildings. Someday while you're here you might like to drive about the island and see some of them. I don't have a car, but Antonio, our village taxi man, could take us."

Gigi said, "I'd love to go, but I doubt that I'll be here long enough. I rather think now that I'll go back early next week. And at this minute"—she had been keeping an eye on the darkening sky—"I think I'd better start back to the house."

At the door, Octavia Milton tucked a little packet of almond cakes into the plastic bag that held Gigi's purchases, and then she embraced her warmly. "Tell Richard that I'll come to call on him soon, perhaps Monday. And—" she hesitated—"please don't think I'm being meddlesome, but I think you should see the lawyer. I can't be certain, but I rather imagine it's Juan Azcona in Sóller, since he's the one most of us use. He speaks perfect English and he could advise you. Why don't you go to see him tomorrow?"

"No. I wouldn't want to risk hurting Richard's feelings by going behind his back, Octavia."

"But there is a possibility that Richard himself may not

know. He may actually be ignorant of the terms of her will."

"She didn't make a will. Richard told me that."

"I'm not for a moment doubting his honesty, but not every wife tells her husband everything she does. You know how your grandmother was. She may not have been quite able to face up to making him unhappy."

Gigi said uncertainly, "That is how she was, but . . ."

"Oh, I'm meddling—yes, there's no other word for it. But she was so definite about wanting you to have the house when we talked that day. In any case, it's something that you should investigate before leaving the island. It might save you the nuisance of having to turn around and come right back."

16

Gigi ran down the winding steps. By the time she reached the square, she had felt a few drops of rain. The taxi sat outside the bar and she could see several men inside playing cards. She opened the door. "Antonio . . .?"

One of the men came toward her. "*Sí, señorita?*"

"Ca'n Cornitx—*por favor?*"

He was a heavy-set, smiling man, but he made no attempt at conversation as they left the little town and then began the steep ascent on the rough road that led up to Ca'n Cornitx. When he came to the washout, where a gully slanted across the road, Antonio spread his big hands and looked around at Gigi, shaking his head. His voice was loud and cheerful, but very definitely he was refusing to drive his big, lumbering car any farther.

"*Muy bien.*" Gigi paid him, said "*Gracias,*" not blaming him at all for not wanting to risk getting stuck here. It was a fairly long city block to the house and now the rain fell steadily, but she did not mind getting a little wet.

This was the first time she had seen the big, sprawling house from this vantage point by daylight. As she hurried up toward it, it looked somber, even ominous, its outlines blurred by the rain. The top of the tower, with those spaced square stones, was like an open mouth from which alternate teeth had been knocked out. She dreaded going back into its cold, bleak darkness.

What if Octavia Milton had been right and Mimi, without Richard's knowledge, had left this house to her? She thought that tomorrow she might go to see the lawyer—Azcona?—after all. Yes, that might be a sensible thing to do, and then if the place had been left to her, she could take whatever legal steps were necessary to give it to Richard. It might make things easier to have the deed already accomplished. Save embarrassment for him. She wouldn't even want to be thanked for the gift of such a cumbersome white elephant.

Hurrying through the courtyard and up the steps to her room, Gigi took a bit of childish pleasure in the knowledge that she had escaped Concepción's watchful eyes and had stolen a bit of freedom for herself. She opened her plastic bag and spread her purchases out on the bed. The olive-wood bowl was all right and she thought the burro rather cute, but now she saw that the cabellero she had bought for Josh was made of plastic, not wood. But she visualized herself giving it to him, felt the way his arms would go around her. *Why* hadn't she let him come? He could have been here by this time tomorrow.

When she had bathed and put on dry clothes, she went downstairs. The lift she had derived from her few hours away from the house was soon dissipated, and the dinner Concepción served in front of the small fire did nothing to cheer her. Leftovers. More loud music. Also, quite obviously, Concepción had been drinking. Gigi caught a whiff of what smelled like whiskey and the woman's color was high. Well, well. *Muy interesante!*

For dessert, she hoped for some of the delicious almond pastry, but she did not know how to ask for it. Concepción brought a collapse of flabby, watery custard. "*Qué es esto?*" Gigi indicated the mess with her spoon.

"*Flan, señorita.*"

"*Oh, muy bien.*"

Concepción's look showed that she thought her a bit of a fool.

Gigi said brightly and fast in English, "Really, it was perfectly awful. The whole meal. You'd not have served it to *him*, that's for sure. I'm puzzled as to why my grandmother has kept you on all these years. You drink a bit too, don't you, with the master away?"

She felt a bit better after her childish outburst, at which Concepción merely nodded and said, "*Gracias, señorita.*"

Poor Concepción. Octavia Milton had said she shouldn't be too hard on her. Gigi wished that she had some of the older woman's compassion. Language barriers were not so great that Gigi could not have by-passed them adequately if Concepción had given her the slightest encouragement, made even one gesture of friendliness. It would have been a welcome diversion now to have gone to the kitchen. She could have offered to wipe the dishes, making do with gestures. Later they could have sat in front of the TV set, laughing together.

But she could not imagine laughing with Concepción. And anyhow, she had a hunch that Concepción might have a date with the bottle.

She made her own selection of records, light, happy tunes that Mimi would have liked, turned the volume low, and sat down to look at the books she had brought from the library this morning. One was a collection of plays. A program fell out. She saw Richard's name in the cast of Ibsen's *A Doll's House*. It had been performed at the Strand Theater in London in 1948.

She could so easily imagine him on the stage. He must have been a good actor. A pity about the knee. She would not have blamed him if he had hated Mimi forever for a thing like that, but apparently he didn't if he could not even remember what the quarrel had been about. Theirs had been one of the love stories in the great tradition, he had said. Or something like that. Ah, well, Gigi knew she didn't know much about love.

Another collection, one of stories by Daphne du Maurier. She read for a while, lost herself. But that writer's calm acceptance of the supernatural made it all too believable to be read in this house on this night. The wind had risen again. It swept down the chimney, scattering ashes. It caused doors to sigh shut.

That sound again. She went over and turned off the music, stood with ears alert. It came again, as if a child were crying. Fear lifted in her breast like a cautioning finger: Listen. It was a bird. Richard had said so. It was foolish to let herself be afraid, but she did not have to stay in this room any longer.

She picked up a last-summer's issue of the French fashion magazine *Elle* from the long table in back of the sofa, turned off the lights, and hurried along the cold corridor and up the long flight of stairs to her room.

She locked her door, kindled a fire, and when it was burning with reassuring cheer, she got the cakes Octavia had given her, and sat, calmly enough, to eat and turn the pages of the magazine. She remembered little of her college French, but she was able to make out most of the captions. The faces of the models were interesting, typical of what she imagined to be the smart Continental look. But styles meant little to her, and it took her very little time to leaf through the magazine.

What could she do now? Write to Josh again and tell him about her good afternoon with her new friend? No, she would be back home before the letter got there. Wash a few clothes? She washed a few clothes. There was no very good place in the bathroom to hang them. In the morning if the sun should shine she might be able to hang them over the balcony.

She picked up the last of the almond cakes—piggish, she knew, but she'd eaten so little at dinner—and went out to look up at the sky. The spasmodic gusts of wind were strong, but a thin wash of moonlight showed her the wild sea, the stunted trees that tossed their arms as if in despair. Curling plumes of white on the waves below caught the light from the moon, lost it, caught it again. Another trance-inducing possibility, she thought, if a person like me were to stand here and watch it long enough.

As she turned to go inside, she heard again that crying, that murmuring, desperate crying.

It was a bird. It was the wind.

It was not a bird. It was not the wind. It was the high,

plaintive crying of a child, with words that were indistinguishable, but unmistakably syllables. It floated, was snatched away by a gust of wind. It seemed to come from the boarded-up part of the house.

Fear lifted in her breast again, like a hand now, raised in a classroom, ready with an answer. She tried to ignore it. Shivering, she waited for a lull in the wind. The cry came again.

I do hear it. This is not my imagination. I am going to go to Concepción, wake her if necessary, demand . . .

She remembered Richard's words: "She was pregnant once . . ." He had not said she'd had the child, only that Mimi had seen her through it.

What if she'd had that child and kept it here in this house to prevent her good Catholic parents from knowing? What if that music, turned up so loud, had been played to keep me from hearing?

Memory filled Gigi's mind with newspaper stories she had read. In California a pitiful case had come to light concerning a child kept in chains for many years. Somewhere in the South two children had been found, emaciated, living in filth like animals in a cellar, unable to speak except in their own gibberish to each other.

No. She would not wake Concepción.

Go. Look. Find the child.

No, she would not go, look, find the child. She was too frightened. She would wait for Richard to come back.

But how could she wait? How could she block out from her mind what might be a pitiful need? How could she sleep?

The stone steps leading down into the courtyard were dim. Her feet, finding themselves there, were unwilling to take her down. But she had to go, had to get to some place in this house where she could listen, satisfy herself that there was not a child somewhere who was in need of her help.

It was none of her business. These days not many people made cries for help their business. She knew it would have been far more sensible to have stayed in her room, pulled the pillow over her ears, and tried to sleep until morning. Then she could have gone looking, managing somehow to search under Concepción's watchful eyes.

But she had to go now. Had to locate the sound, try to make out the words, if they were words.

Gigi hurried across the courtyard where the servants, all those years ago, had laughed and talked loudly while her mother above had screamed and plunged to her death.

In the salon, she stood in front of the dying fire, trying to warm herself, trying to get back her ebbing courage. Up there on the balcony, dim now in the last glow of the fire, something, somebody had appeared on that night. And then disappeared in a swift flurry of movement that had been crazily reflected in the silver urn. Had it been that child who had been dragged back? She would not, could not, go up those stairs.

Wishing she had a flashlight, she picked up the candle from the table, lit it, slipped the packet of matches in her pocket, and shielding the flame with one hand, went up the stairs. Cautiously, she turned the knob on the door to the right, opened it a little. She could just listen.

The door was jerked from her hand, slamming back against the wall as a sudden, howling draft rampaged through the house, making the hangings on the wall billow as if they were alive, the rugs on the floor lift a little as if things lived under them.

Nonsense. Balderdash. Somewhere a window must have

blown open, or a door, creating suction. Or maybe it was just the wind coming down the great chimney in the salon, mad with glee to have found, with this opening door, a way to fill the whole house with its strength, burst out the walls from within.

With an effort Gigi forced the door shut. It was best not to venture up there, since she was not sure where the sound came from. Her candle flame was gone. She took the packet of matches from her pocket, lit the candle again. In the comparative quiet she listened, looking around her on the balcony.

A crackled old mirror showed her reflection. She was not unlike a witch herself, with her pale hair all wild, her face shadowy and distorted. She put her ear to the door to listen, leaning close.

It came again, the sound for which she had been straining her ears. A pitiful, keening babble of syllables that sounded vaguely Spanish. Not the wind. No bird ever cried like that, talking. Her scalp tightened. The hot wax from the candle fell on her hand and she tilted it at an angle so that the drops fell on the rug.

Never mind about the rug. The sounds came clearly from above, up those steps beyond the doorway where she stood. They came from the room where Richard had said a nursery used to be.

Gigi pulled open the door, holding it firm in case another draft should try to snatch it from her hand again. She closed it, started up the stairs. Halfway up, she stopped and stood motionless to listen. The sound was more distinct, low-key now, the fretful moaning of a sick child. She visualized the room at the top of the stairs, its boarded windows, fallen ceiling. Anger rose, crowding out fear.

She ran up the rest of the stairs, lifted her hand to knock.

Her mind formed the words: *Let me come in.* But she did not say the words, did not knock. Concepción might be in there. She would not let her in. She grasped the knob, turning it with slow care. She would take just a peek.

The door was locked. She was not meant to go into this room.

But she meant to go in.

The key. It was logical to suppose that it was the one she had seen hidden in the rice canister. Hidden from her—who else?—on the chance she should go prowling.

She felt a little reckless. While Mimi was alive and in possession of all her faculties, she never would have allowed a child, any creature, to suffer in her house. Mimi, for all her faults, had been kind. When had the child been brought here? Probably after Mimi's death, or after she was too sick to be aware of what was going on.

Dripping candle wax, she hurried down the stairs, knowing that the fresh drops of wax would be noticed by the next person—Concepción—who came up these stairs. Gigi didn't care much. If she found it to be true that a neglected child lay in that room that was open to the elements in this cold, windy, rainy weather, she intended to go, first thing in the morning, to Son Baraitx and get in touch with the proper authorities. Octavia Milton would help her.

Richard. What about his part in all this? Surely he must have known about this. She tried to blank out her mind, let pure outrage take over. Answers could come later, and she'd not mind confronting him with whatever she found out.

Concepción. She was something else. There was a barrier there that went beyond language or culture. Something in that dark, handsome face frightened Gigi a little.

The candle flickered and went out more than once in her

hurried flight down the stairs. She tiptoed as she approached the kitchen, not knowing quite what she would do if Concepción should be there. The kitchen was dark. She snapped on the light. Concepción was not there. She blew out her candle and set it down.

One glance showed her that the room did not have its usual neatness. Dishes and pans were piled in the sink. Gigi remembered her earlier suspicion that Concepción had been drinking.

She opened the rice canister. Her fingers encountered only rice, no key. Dismayed, she looked about the kitchen with its hundreds of other possible hiding places and tried to think. Where would Concepción, most logically, have put it? Even if she had been a little bit drunk, she probably would have had sense enough to put it in a place where it was not likely to be found.

If she'd had her wits about her at all, she would have kept it on her person. Probably, right now, it was in the pocket of the white apron that she wore over her black uniform.

Gigi looked about the kitchen, hoping that she might see the apron hanging over the back of a chair or on one of the hooks by the back door. A dishtowel lay on the back of a chair. A coat, head scarf, and straw shopping basket hung on the hooks by the back door. No apron was in sight.

The apron would be in Concepción's room. Gigi felt as if there were a fist now in her chest, hammering. She stepped out into the passage that she knew led to Concepción's room, but she did not know which of the several doors was the right one. She opened one that led downward and closed it hastily, remembering the snake and not in any mood to have the thing come slithering toward her. She opened a door that led into a pantry, another into a storeroom. She stopped by the door at the end and now she could hear the rhythmic sounds of snoring. No knob was on this door, only a latch. Gigi lifted it, stepped into the room. Behind her, the latch fell with a clatter as the wind sucked the door noisily shut.

The snoring stopped. The girl stood motionless, scarcely breathing, not daring to take a step backward that might betray her. The anger that had sustained her now faltered a little. How would she find the Spanish to explain her presence here? But as she sought for the words she might have to use, the snoring began again. The room was heavy with the fumes of liquor.

In the dimness, a blur of white showed in a tumble of dark clothes on a chair beside the bed. With quick, soft steps Gigi moved, reached for the blur of white, her fingers fumbling for the pocket. The key, long and heavy. Her fingers closed around it, drew it out. She put it in her own pocket. Then, her eyes on the figure on the bed, she stepped backward, lifted the latch with care, and eased it back as she shut the door behind her.

Pick up the candle in the kitchen again. Light it. Hurry. Don't stop to think.

Outside the door on the top floor, she stopped. No sound came now from the other side of the door. It might be sleeping. *It.* Suppose that whatever was in there was really an *it.* Not a normal child, but some poor, crazed, subhuman thing that might come dragging itself toward her across the floor through the fallen plaster. A *thing* that had to be kept locked in here because it could not be released, might even be dangerous.

Her hand shook as she inserted the key in the lock. It seemed to fit. She was sure it would open the door. But maybe it would be best not to open this door, not to look.

191

She had never been one to pay for the horrors of viewing side-show freaks. She had thrown up one time after a biology-class tour through a medical lab where evidence of nature's mistakes, formaldehyde-preserved, stood on shelves in big jars.

Be sensible. Take the key out of the lock without turning it. Go back to Concepción's room and replace it in the apron pocket. Climb then up to your room, sleep—or not sleep—until morning, when it will be possible to communicate with somebody who will know what to do.

As she was about to withdraw the key from the lock, she heard that plaintive, murmuring moaning, then a gasping sound of pain. Her fingers cold and unsteady, Gigi opened the door a very little.

The room was warm, that was her first sensation, not bitter and blowing with cold rain. It was lighted too. Dimly, but with more light than would have come from the pale moonlight.

The moaning had stopped. She pushed the door open a little more, one eye close to the crack that permitted her to view a narrow slice of the room, from the carved gold-and-white of the rug, up a damask-covered wall where she could see the edge of a gold-framed picture, to the ceiling that was beamed and whole, with plaster intact. She pushed the door open a little further until she could see half the room. Furniture now, elegant little chairs with tufted yellow velvet, tables of chrome and glass. The edge of a canopied bed.

Gigi flung the door wide, stepped into the warm, beautiful room, the rug thick under her feet. On the bed, looking toward her, was a small witch.

No, an old child.

No. The halo of gray hair was tipped with flame. It was Mimi.

17

"Mimi . . .?" Gigi stumbled across the room. Eyes peered. The mouth opened in the wasted face. "Who . . .? Yes, yes . . ." Arms—bones loosely draped with skin—lifted to embrace. The girl knelt, hiding her face as her stunned mind fought against shock for comprehension.

Richard told me you were dead. I saw your grave. She choked back the words.

Fingers like bird claws combed through the blond hair. "My little Gigi. It's really you."

"Yes. It's me."

"I wandered in my sleep. They try to keep me from wan-

dering because I fall—I fall and get such bruises." Her
words were slow, a little slurred. "It's this silly thing that
ails me. But I saw . . . I thought I saw you down there by
the fire. Concepción carried me back to bed. She told me I
had dreamed . . ."

Gigi could believe it was her grandmother's voice as long
as she didn't look at her face. She said, her voice muffled
against a down-filled puff, "It wasn't a dream."

"I do dream things. Strange, weird. My mind—from all
the drugs—plays tricks. But I had to know if I really saw
you. So part of the time—part of the time—I've not been
taking my pain capsules. I suppose they thought I wasn't up
to seeing you just yet. I've been so ill. The pain—oh, God,
the pain. I've screamed with it, cried like a silly baby. I
could never stand pain. But I had to try—to try to clear my
mind. Find out what was real."

What was real? Not Richard's tears, his choked account
of Mimi's death. (*I thought she just needed to rest. I said,
"Sleep, darling . . ."*)

Gigi lifted her head, her eyes going about the room. This
beautiful room hardly seemed real, so firmly had she fixed it
in her mind as a wind-swept, dangerous place of wet, falling
plaster.

She saw a low stool and pulled it close to the bed. She
made herself smile into the face that bore so little resem-
blance to the one she had seen last summer, every summer.
She caught hold of the reaching, feverish hands, forcing
brightness. "I am here. I am really here. I came as soon as I
got your cablegram."

"Cablegram?"

"You sent one, didn't you, telling me to come?"

"I sent . . . ? Rich must have sent it. To surprise me. But
that was naughty of him not to have told me. I'd have

slipped into Palma to get my hair done if I'd known you were coming. But I guess he thought it would be nice if you spent Christmas . . ."

Christmas?

"Or is it spring? Never mind. The days have no meaning. They keep the place so dark, I don't know day from night." She frowned, said like a fretful child, "Richard had that done to the windows the other day—I don't know why. Hammering, pounding, when rest is what I need. My doctor said I had to rest to be ready for you in the spring. And I've been such a good girl, just resting, resting, to get over this foolish thing. Move the light, darling. I look so ghastly without make-up."

Gigi reached to move the light so that it did not shine so mercilessly on the emaciated face.

"I can tell that you are wondering—*no es verdad?* I fell, you see. Yes, I am sure that must have been what started this whole wretched business. I think I broke something inside me. It's taken quite some time to heal. That's what hurts so, the healing. That shows it's getting better—my gizzard, or whatever the hell it was I broke." She laughed gaily, that breathy, little-girl laugh of hers, then clutched her middle and rolled over. "I must not . . . must not give in with you here."

Gigi was on her feet. "Let me get you something for the pain."

"Not yet. Wait. *Momentito*—it will go. I can tell the ones that won't last. I don't want to be put to sleep, now that you have just come. We must talk, make plans." She half sat up, panting as she made an effort at control. "Ah, yes. There, now. It is easing. I'll be all right for a few minutes. You be careful, *carissima*, that you don't ever fall and break anything inside of you."

"I'll be careful. Oh, Mimi, are you sure you have a doctor who is . . . ?"

"Oh, yes. A precious man. *Mais oui.* The best in Palma. He advised against an operation—thank God for small favors."

"But shouldn't you be in a hospital now where they can . . . ?"

"No, never. People die in hospitals. This is where I want to be. Richard and Concepción are such good nurses. Angels, both of them, so sweet to me. They can't bear to have me suffer. But Concepción keeps the bottle of my pain capsules so that I won't accidentally take too many— they're both so afraid something will happen to me."

Gigi tried to think of sensible words. "I'm glad they're so good to you."

"Yes, yes. Oh, Concepción just gets frantic when I cry. She's been giving me extra capsules to quiet me these last few days—two, three—I lose track of time. But I've not taken them. I've hidden them in a little box in the drawer of my bedside table with the rosary she gave me. Such a good Catholic, my Concepción. Such a faithful friend. She rubs me, bathes me, files my nails, coaxes me to eat. Not a word of English, so it will be hard for you to get to know her. But Rich, my darling Richard, has he charmed you?"

"Yes." *He told me you were dead and I believed him. He cried at your grave and I believed his tears. I visualized Brother Antonio at your funeral, the villagers with their flowers.* "Yes, Richard has charmed me."

"And he's brilliant. I admire brilliance. I'm such a feather-brain! I've always known that he has—and quite rightly—rather a contempt for my mind and for the minds of almost everybody!" She laughed. The flesh had melted back from her mouth so that her teeth looked large and long and frightening.

Gigi said, "Yes, I know he is brilliant."

"But no saint, my Ricardo. I'd never have lived with a saint. He was naughty once with Concepción. Can you believe it? *Es verdad.* I punished him for that. Gave him a crack across the knee so he'd never forget. But I was naughty too"—she rolled her sunken eyes, her coquettish smile a ghastly travesty—"and with more than one! But I always came back to my Richard."

Reality. Was it anywhere? Gigi still clutched for a straw of it, unable to think of a question that would provide an answer she could cling to.

"And my Ca'n Cornitx—you love that too?"

"It's . . . it's so much more like a castle than I ever dreamed. So big."

"And very valuable, too, in today's market. Sell it to some rich American if it's too much for you, my angel. Or to a Japanese—they're the ones now who have all the money. I've had fantastic offers. The house will be yours, of course, when I die—which will be *years* from now, I promise you. Still, one must plan."

"But Richard said—I mean, I had supposed he would be the one who . . ."

"No, my baby, no. I've made that clear in my will. My sweet Richard has had quite enough from me. It will not be his. Unless you should predecease me. I let them add that little paragraph—let me see, when was it?—quite recently. My lawyer came from Sóller. It seemed to make Richard happy. I like to have everybody happy. And it doesn't really matter, only a formality, not worth worrying about. It's hardly likely that you will predecease me."

Hardly likely in the real world of order and logic. But this was not the real world. Gigi sat very still, trying to force her thoughts to be orderly, logical, against a rising tide of fear.

Her grandmother's voice went on, a disconnected rambling of words that the girl did not try to follow. She looked into the dying face. Yes, dying. Mimi might not be able to face reality after all the years of avoiding it, but I must face it, Gigi thought. I must try to think what to do.

Go to Son Baraitx the first thing in the morning. Run up all those steps to Octavia Milton's house. Tell her everything, get her advice. Call Josh Lincoln, say come, come quickly.

"Don't look so worried, *querida*. What is there to worry about? I'll be up and out of this wretched bed in no time at all, now that you're here. You will stay until spring, of course. We'll tear up the island. You and I will go visiting all the lovely people and—" She stopped, caught her breath, and sat up to lean, clutching her folded arms close as she rocked back and forth.

Gigi had jumped to her feet. "Mimi—oh, Mimi. We've talked now—you know I'm really here. Let me help you. Let me get you something for the pain."

She gasped, "Yes. Two of my capsules, please. Oh, my God, do hurry. This is—I can always tell—going to be one of the worst ones." She sucked breath between clenched teeth, waved toward the bedside table. "There."

Gigi fumbled in the drawer, pushing aside some tissues, a small flashlight, to get at the little box with the tangled rosary and a few capsules.

She placed two of them in the outstretched, shaking hand, poured water from a carafe that sat on the table, held the glass and supported the skeletal frame while Mimi gulped.

The eyes rolled upward, wild with pain. "It's a knife twisting inside me, reaming me. Don't leave me, Gigi. Wait. The capsules will help pretty soon." Moaning, giving those little cries the girl had heard before, Mimi twisted sideways, doubled up, and fell back against the pillows.

Feeling helpless, Gigi paced the beautiful room, the warmth almost stifling with its heavy scent of Joy. All the windows were covered with thick draperies. She pushed one aside, thinking to let in a breath of air, then saw the boards nailed on the outside. She had forgotten.

But her memory, like a tape recording in her head, played back what Richard had told her: *The ceiling is falling in. I have locked the door so Concepción won't take it into her head to go in and try to sweep up the mess. The house is mine, of course. I'll hang on with my dying breath.*

She opened doors. One led to a bathroom, extravagantly fitted with gold-colored fixtures. Another one, louvered, opened into a walk-in closet that held what must be thousands of dollars' worth of clothes, all in the bright pastel colors Mimi loved. One dress was coral cashmere, high-necked, long-sleeved, warm . . .

When the moaning on the bed had quieted, Gigi went back to sit on the stool again. With gentle fingers she smoothed back the wild gray hair. It was damp with sweat, but the tips were shining and bright as the end of summer.

Mimi said in a tired voice, "It's so good when it stops. I get, for a few minutes, such a lovely high, like three martinis. It lets me think very clearly before the drowsiness begins. It takes the edge off all my little worries, makes everything quite bearable. Put the capsules in the drawer where I can find them easily, darling."

There were six left. Gigi placed the little box at the front of the drawer, closed it.

Her grandmother reached for her hands, feeling of them as if she might not be able to see very well. "Your hands, darling, they're so awful, as if you might char for a living. And your nails are all broken. Don't tell me you've started biting them again. The ring! The ring I sent you—why aren't you wearing it?"

"It's at the jeweler's, being made larger. Mimi, I'll wear it just as soon . . ."

The sunken eyes seemed to look on another scene. "Papa gave that diamond ring to Mama when he started making all that money. Back when I was Maisie Heidelreich. Don't ever tell anybody I was ever Maisie Heidelreich."

"I won't."

"Let me hear you laugh, Gigi. I've not heard that wonderful laugh of yours one single time. How you used to laugh when you were a baby! You were everybody's pet. I remember the way you used to beg Richard for a ride on his shoulders."

"He said I used to call him Dickie."

"No, no, why would he say that? I don't remember what you called him, but nobody ever called him Dickie. Your mother, of course, seldom called him by name, seldom spoke to him. But then, she hated him. Oh, why can't everybody love everybody? He knew she hated him, knew she was trying to get me to give him up. If I hadn't seen him running up from the beach right after she fell . . ."

Gigi's eyes were wide. "Are you saying that you thought that Richard had something to do with . . . ?"

"No, no. Don't look like that, darling. The police investigated very thoroughly. Her door was locked from the inside. Ever since your letter came, I've been racking my poor brain for some way to explain . . . Maybe she just got dizzy out there."

Gigi knew the balcony railing was too high for that to provide a sensible explanation, but she said hungrily, "You mean you think she may not have done it deliberately?" There might not be much time left to satisfy her craving for every crumb of consolation.

"She couldn't have. She was such a wonderful mother, my beautiful Ann, so much better than I ever was. You were her life. She had such plans for you. It must have been an accident. One must always try to believe the best, darling. That's what I've tried to do."

"I know, Mimi."

"And don't dig into the past, sweet child. All that is best forgotten. Don't let yourself be hypno—hypnotized again, regressed . . ." Her words had started slurring a little. She sighed and smiled a little, looking beyond Gigi's eyes. "I think . . . think maybe you had a balloon, my baby. She leaned, my Ann, to catch it when you let it go. And when it floated . . . floated . . ." Mimi's voice was floating. "I love balloons. We'll buy some. We'll blow them up and have a party. Yes. A lovely party with balloons." Her eyes were closing. "We'll have lovely times. You'll stay. And in the spring . . . or is it spring?"

"Not yet." Gigi held her grandmother's hand, letting the tears pour down her cheeks. She knew there would not be another spring.

"In the morn—the morning . . ."

"Yes. In the morning we'll talk some more. I'm going now so that you can sleep. I'm borrowing your flashlight, okay?"

The frail hand on the bed lifted in a little wave. *"Hasta . . . hasta mañana."*

Gigi took the little flashlight, painted with flowers, from the drawer of the bedside table. She leaned to touch her grandmother's forehead with her lips. She whispered, "Goodnight."

Mimi was breathing heavily, but if she heard her, she gave no sign.

18

Lock Mimi's door. Go down the stairs. Go into Concepción's room again and replace the key in the apron pocket.

Gigi gave herself simple directions, and like a simple child, she began obeying them. She was as much afraid to pause and try to evaluate the dangers of a misstep now as a tightrope walker who must make it to safety without a net.

Lies, all lies, she had been told by Richard. She knew there was no safety for her in this house.

After Mimi's overheated room, the house felt very cold. The wind had died down and each sound she made seemed very loud to her ears. The flashlight's beam was feeble, as if the battery might be about to go. She turned it off when she got down the dark stairs to the balcony level, for the moon was casting wavering shadows as it tried to break through the clouds.

There on the stairs that led down to the salon, something wavered, seemed to glide. It was only the shadow of the curving stair rail, but she had gasped when she sighted it and dropped the flashlight, so that now it clattered noisily, hitting every one of the tiled steps before it reached the bottom. For as much as a minute she stood motionless at the top of the stairs, half expecting a light to be turned on below.

Fool. She said the word to herself bitterly. There was no snake. Only a fool would have believed that wild story of Richard's about the snake. He had told her that only to keep her from prowling. He had contempt for other people's minds, Mimi had said. At the moment Gigi shared the contempt he must have had for hers. Even Concepción, not bright, must have sneered if he had confided the snake story to her.

She picked up the flashlight at the bottom of the stairs, relieved to find that it still had a bit of its gleam, and then, a little reckless, knowing that drunk Concepción would not be wakened by footsteps, she went quickly through the salon, back through the kitchen and the stone-floored passage that led to Concepción's room.

Gigi listened for a moment, her ear against the door. The drunken snoring noises had stopped and were replaced by the heavy, but more normal, sounds of a sleeper's breathing. Remembering the loud click the latch had made before, she opened it with care, eased it back into place, before she tiptoed to the chair to pick up the white apron. She slipped the big key back into the pocket and glanced toward the bed, made more visible now by the moonlight.

On one of the bed posts at the head, a vine seemed to be growing. Thick, twining. It moved a little, slithering. With a hoarse, indrawn breath, Gigi stepped backward, remembering brave words she had spoken. They were untrue. She was almost paralyzed by atavistic horror, scarcely able to move backward toward the door, her eyes fixed on the snake.

A clattering ring, just as she reached the door and was about to slip through it. A groan of protest from the bed, a muttering as Concepción seemed to be trying to shut off the alarm. A crash as the clock struck the floor, still ringing.

While the bell continued its strident sound, Gigi ducked through the door, easing the latch behind her with as much care as her fright would permit. She ran, not for a moment now believing that snakes did not chase people. In this terrible house, anything could happen.

Up in her room, she locked her door, got into bed with her clothes on, and gave way to shuddering panic.

She was sure that the alarm clock had been set to alert Concepción to her nursing duties. Probably by now she had been able to rouse herself enough to go upstairs and check on the invalid. Mimi would surely be too sedated to give anything away, but what if Concepción should notice the absence of the flashlight, the trail of spilled candle wax?

What did I do with the candle? Did I leave it up there on Mimi's bedside table? More panic, until a bulge in her pocket told her that she had put it there without thinking. She must think from now on. Surely it would not be too hard to outthink Concepción.

How deeply was Concepción into all this? She and Richard had been—one time, at least, a thousand times for all Gigi cared—"naughty" together. Richard must have involved her in the scheme from its beginning. She could imagine that he might have described her as a scheming little American who was coming to cheat him out of his rights to Ca'n Cornitx. Clever Richard. Dull-witted Concepción, who would believe anything, do anything, very likely, to get to be a movie star.

But what was Concepción supposed to do between now and Saturday? Gigi did not intend to wait to find out. In the morning, very early, she was getting out of this house.

What if Concepción, bigger than she, certainly stronger, should try to stop her? Fervently, Gigi wished she had stuck with the karate lessons until she had attained more proficiency. Avoid Concepción in the morning, that was the thing to do. Take no chances on being seen. It might even be wise not to go by the road, just make her way over the mountain in the direction of Son Baraitx.

Her feet were cold. She reached for the heavy wool bedspread and drew it over the blankets. She had to get warm enough to sleep for a little while. Rest and a clear head would be needed for tomorrow.

What if Richard *had* killed her mother? She wished Mimi hadn't put that idea into her head when she already had too much to cope with. But was there a chance that a sleepy little girl, awakening from her nap, could have seen him in this room, connecting him somehow with a witch—dark clothes, perhaps, some sort of disguise?

No. Richard could not have been in this room. They had seen him on the beach. Concepción was the most likely candidate for the role of witch, but she had been with the other servants below. Forget Concepción, that sinister woman with her sinister dark pet twining. Gigi was shaking all over, still cold. She must be having a nervous chill, maybe coming down with something. No. She refused to be ill. She would be all right if she could just sleep for a while.

She tried to count sheep. Visualized them running up the side of that same mountain which she would climb tomorrow to get away from this house, where unbelievably, but almost surely, a scheme was under way to kill her.

"Richard . . ." She groaned the name out loud. She had been taken in by him so completely, felt such a rapport. Was there still some good, simple explanation that would put him in the clear?

He was smart. He must know he could never get away with contriving her death to precede Mimi's. But why else would he have brought her here with that urgent cablegram? Why else would he have hidden the fact that Mimi still lived?

No answers. Just the chilling memory of Mimi's words: *The house will be yours . . . It's hardly likely that you will predecease me.*

Hardly likely. Damned unlikely, Gigi told herself grimly, now that I am forewarned. She tossed, wondering if she had been incredibly stupid not to have picked up some warning clues before. Richard's sweet, friendly face loomed, taunting her. How moved she had been by his easy tears, that naked sorrow, those tender lines of reminiscence!

Fury possessed her, pushing sleep even further away. How had Richard hidden his amusement at her gullibility? What a pity that his performance had been limited to an audience of one—it could have won some kind of award! She must even have said the lines he intended her to say!

That must have been the grave of Carlos, Octavia Milton's gardener, that she had seen in the cemetery, where Richard had said he would plant one of the flowering trees that Mimi loved. With his dramatist's appreciation for convincing detail, it must have pleased him no end to be able to add that splendid bit of realism.

Her churning mind dredged up something else. What about her narrow escape on the beach? Had she almost provided him with an easy way to get rid of her? She remembered the boulder she had dodged. Until this moment she had thought she dislodged it by tugging at the tree root, but now she wondered if Richard might have given the rock a push. He could easily have done so when he saw her struggling upward to escape the sea. Her battered, drowned body could have been found the next day by the police, the coast guard, or whatever help one summoned on this island.

And why had Richard gone to the mainland? Had a boy really come with a message saying he was urgently needed? It might have been just another of his lies, or it might have been true, necessitating a postponement of his plans for her.

She could come up with no sensible answers. She knew only that she must get some sleep and escape this house early in the morning.

19

T*he* door was locked. The bolt had been pushed from
the other side sometime while Gigi had slept past
the dawn light she had counted on to waken her. She beat
on the door, rattled it, screamed for Concepción.

She expected no answer and there was none. More baffled and angry at the moment than scared, Gigi went out on
the balcony to look at the bright sun that smiled now on the
blue sea. It was still chilly, but the calm brilliance of the day
gave truth to the travel promoters' promises that lured the
sun-starved vacationers to these shores.

Could she get out of here by knotting the sheets and
blankets together? There were not enough of them. She
looked down onto the jagged rocks and shuddered at the

cruel distance that made such a scheme impossible. She was not going to risk following her mother to that kind of death.

The pigeons cooed with a sound like water being poured from a bottle, a monotonous sound that they made over and over. They clapped upward, celebrating the arrival of the splendid day.

Somebody might come. A delivery boy. Tourists, even, some of the hardy Germans or Scandinavians, used to cold, to hiking, might wander this far from the guidebooks' suggestions.

Nobody came. Concepción made no sound to indicate she was even in this house. Very likely she had seen the candle drippings, or Mimi might have told her. It had not occurred to Gigi to caution her grandmother to keep her visit a secret, so sure had she been that by early morning she would be away from here safely.

She called Mimi's name until she was hoarse. Mimi, if she still lived, gave no sign, did not cry now. Without much hope, the girl stared toward the boarded windows. Even if that frail, dying woman heard her, what could she do to help her?

With the fruit knife from the bowl that had held oranges, she worked at the crack in the door. But that also was without hope. She could not budge that heavy bolt on the other side.

Midday came. While the pigeons gurgled and flew, irridescent in the sun, she sat on the balcony in her bathing suit, refusing to dwell on the thought that her co-workers might never see her tan. She dwelt on her hunger, rather than her fear. She wished she had not eaten all of those almond cakes last night. How outrageous it was of Concepción not to bring her some food! That erring husband had been let out of this room after a week, penitent. A *week!* But she was sure Concepción had locked her in here only to keep her out of mischief until Richard came back.

Except for the narrow beach, the coast, awesome in its harsh beauty, stretched in rocky gray cliffs as far as she could see on either side. There was no sign whatever of human habitation, no smoke rising, no sounds except for those made by the pigeons and the sea birds and the waves, and occasionally, the distant tinkle of a sheep bell.

Once she thought she heard a donkey bray. Gigi watched the road, hoping that a driver might come into sight, bringing a load of wood or something to the house. No one came up the road. She did not hear the donkey bray again.

In spite of the cool air, she knew she was getting too much sun, so she went inside for tanning lotion. Back at Dulles, her friends were envying her this sun, never dreaming she was being held prisoner. *Say the word,* Josh Lincoln had said, *and I'll be there.* And she had said *Stay.*

One hope seemed valid and she clung to it: Octavia Milton might tell someone of Mimi's "death." She remembered that Octavia had told her she intended to plunge right in and finish the book and not even answer the door. But she held the thought, trying to look, as Mimi would have done, on the bright side. It was, she knew, not awfully bright.

The pigeons cooed on. No longer was she reminded of gurgling water being poured from a bottle. It was only an annoying, repetitive sound being made by idiot birds.

The sun was setting, turning the sky to shining gold, then purple that deepened into lavender-gray, the wrinkling sea reflecting the changing clouds. Gigi did not let herself fantasize, imagining scenes that did not exist in the cloud shapes. Shadows crept, amethyst, mauve, becoming black when the moon came out, an imperfect circle. The stars, pointy little diamonds, shivered in the deep, dark sky.

She had brought her coat and she sat there huddled in it for a long time. The scent of almond blossoms came from somewhere, reminding her of that night when, under the spell of Richard's voice, she had been charmed to hear that Majorca floated like a basket of flowers on the sea.

A couple of lights appeared in the lower part of the house. Now Mimi's voice came to her, crying like a child. Feeling helpless, Gigi stood listening. She screamed, "Mimi . . . Mimi!" And then, "Concepción! Concepción, let me out of here!"

Her voice came back to her, echoed from the walls of the house, from the cliffs and the mountain.

Nobody answered.

She went inside, tried to read the dull books, looked again at the French magazine. She took a bath and did her nails, even putting bright polish on them, thinking with dreary humor that her corpse, if they killed her, was going to look like that of a typical American tourist who cared quite a lot about grooming.

It had been a long day. She'd had little sleep the night before, so she slept. She dreamed that she lay in a casket, covered with, smothered with, the sick-sweet funeral smell of lilies. She fought to breathe, turning her head from side to side to free herself from the suffocation of the padded satin lining of the casket lid as it was being pressed, held down tightly against her face.

She lunged, fought free of the pressure of the fabric. Could see now the dark, witchlike figure that loomed above her. She gasped, caught breath, gave a shout, and thrust the side of her hand upward in a desperate karate chop against the dimly glimpsed throat. The figure choked, gagged, staggered backward toward the closet door. The door closed.

Gigi sat on the side of the bed, groggy, gasping for

enough good air to clear her head. The fumes of those terrible lilies still lingered in the room. No, not lilies, but chloroform, ether. She reached for the bedside lamp, felt the cord give way as she wrenched it from the socket in the wall.

Eyes on the closet door, she got to her feet, stood waiting, wavering a little as she breathed hard and hoped she would be strong enough to use the heavy lamp as a weapon. She moved closer, her fingers tight on the lamp, waiting for the crack to widen, the door to move outward, the figure to reappear. Those choking, gagging sounds, she was sure, had come from a woman's throat.

Nothing moved. The moonlight was pale and steady on the door. When the waiting was unbearable, Gigi tiptoed forward to listen. No sound of breathing or any movement came from the closet. She knew that a sharp blow on the throat could immobilize, or even kill, but she was sure that even in her desperation she had not been able to exert enough force for that.

Holding the lamp high, ready to bring it down with all her strength, she reached for the knob, took a firm grip, and jerked it open.

The closet was empty. Her few clothes swayed a little on their hangers. She opened the other door. The mirror over the dressing table reflected a shadowy image that startled her until she realized it was her own. She set the lamp down and then, foolishly, she moved the dresses aside, feeling, looking, unable to believe the closet was empty. The shelf above held nothing but her suitcase.

She stepped back, looking around the room to see if there might be another hiding place, unable to believe she was alone. The bathroom was on the same side. She might have been confused about the door. With the lamp grasped tightly, she jerked the bathroom door open. No one was there.

She was not cold, but she was trembling. She sank down on the bed. The smell, not unlike a profusion of funeral flowers, still lingered in the dark room. Or was it only her imagination? Had she only been having one of her dreams? Nothing remained to prove otherwise, unless there really was that odor that might be chloroform or ether.

It was entirely possible that she had had a very vivid nightmare, complete with smell, sight, and sound. Her experiences in this house had been enough to induce any kind of hallucination.

She had not turned on the light, but now she went to the wall switch and snapped it on, bringing the objects in the room into brightness that hurt her eyes for a moment as she looked about at the tumbled bed, the open closet doors.

Her door was still locked from the inside. She unlocked it and pushed, but the bolt on the outside was still in place. Crossing the room for a look at the floor-length windows, she found them just as she had left them, open a little, held outward by the long iron latches that hooked in such a way as to hold them ajar a few inches. No one could have come through the windows even if it had been possible to scale the wall outside.

Unless her senses had failed her completely—and she began to wonder if they had—the dark figure had disappeared into the closet. Again she examined it, this time motivated by the remembered stories of old houses that had secret panels that slid if you pressed the right place.

The closet had no panels. Gigi moved her hands over the plastered walls behind her clothes. In a couple of places the plaster had fallen away, revealing the stones. But the walls were solid, with no cracks that would allow anything to move or swing outward, or whatever it was that such walls were supposed to do. The shelf over her clothes was firm. She tugged at it, although she could see that it was bolted solidly to the wall.

Half-heartedly now, she knelt to run her fingers all over the red shag rug on the floor to see if there might be seams that would reveal the presence of a trap door. She found no seams, no bump to indicate an iron ring that might be tugged upward.

It was almost four o'clock. Soon it would be dawn. She turned off the overhead light, got back into bed, calling herself a fool and telling herself she had to try to sleep. Please God, without nightmares.

The pigeons, clapping upward, awakened her. She got up and went to stand on the balcony to look at the unbelievable blue of the sea. The birds out there circled, shining against the sky, their screams not quite so angry. She wished she had their gift of flight. It would even be rather good to be able to dive into the water and bring up a fish. She was so hungry.

Richard would come back today. All he wanted was this house. She would promise, sign anything, if he would just let her be with Mimi and then let her off this island. She visualized herself working again behind the airline counter, kidding with Carol, listening to the gossip, feeling Josh's hands giving her surreptitious little pats as he moved past her.

Probably she loved him. Whether she did or not, she would marry him in a minute if he ever asked her again. They would have a safe little house somewhere, children. She would join a car pool and go to P.T.A. and do all those corny things that Mimi had turned her back upon. She would get to know his parents, find out what a dahlia looked like.

I am a square now. Now when it's too late to do me any good, I am beginning to know what I want and who I could be.

Sure, sure. Promises, promises. The kind people made and seldom kept, sniveling on their knees to God when they thought they faced death. She didn't think she faced death. Richard, for all his lies, had sense enough to know he couldn't get away with murdering her. She would go with him to Mimi, get her to sign whatever it was one signed. They could have the lawyer come out here and do it all in a legal way that would leave no loopholes. Concepción, damn her, could be the witness.

Gigi brushed her teeth. The toothpaste was minty, sweet and delicious. She could understand why children sometimes ate it. Those with dietary deficiencies ate all manner of peculiar things. I have a dietary deficiency, she thought. I could eat almost anything.

Maybe this morning Concepción would relent and bring her some breakfast. She dressed in sweater and jeans again, listening for sounds outside her door.

The sound she heard was a motor starting up at the back of the house. She dashed to the window and looked out. Concepción was driving away in the truck. Gigi screamed and screamed. The truck kept on going.

She screamed toward the boarded windows for Mimi. Mimi had been able to get out of bed that one time and come down the stairs as far as the balcony. She yelled until her voice gave out, but there was no reply. She knew it had been hopeless anyhow. Mimi might be able to get out of bed, but she would never be able to climb forty-eight steps to get to this room and slide back the bolt. With no telephone, there was no way for her to get in touch with the outside world for help.

Gigi worked again with the little knife at the crack in the door, looked at the big bolted hinges. The iron strips on the door were ornamented with round dots, and over them curving half-circles that seemed to lift, like raised eyebrows, in surprise that she would even try.

Frustrated, she started to make up her bed, since there was nothing else whatever to do. She saw it then, a torn square of wine-colored satin, padded, as if it had been part of an old bathrobe. It was in the bedclothes at the foot of the bed. She held it to her nose and the faint sick-sweet smell re-created her nightmare.

It had not been a nightmare. Someone had come to this room. Someone had really tried to kill her. Who else but Concepción? Concepción, whose alarm clock had been set night before last. Suppose it hadn't been set to waken her to the invalid's needs, but to come here, upon Richard's instructions. But she had been drinking, Gigi remembered, quite likely to get up her courage, and then, dead drunk, had slept through. Last night she had come and made the attempt. And then had vanished.

Nobody vanishes. Concepción wasn't a witch who could say magic words and take off on a broom through the air.

Gigi went back into the closet. She turned on the bulbs around the mirror and looked up at the ceiling, which she had not thought to examine the night before. But there were only the endings of the beams from the bedroom ceiling, and they were solidly plastered into place. They gave not at all when she stood on the dressing-table bench and pushed upward with all her strength.

She knelt again, probing the red shag carpet, every inch

of it this time. Her fingers encountered a slit at the end wall, slipped into it. She tugged upward. Half the floor of the little closet moved. It made no sound. The carpeting seemed to be cemented to some sort of thin wood, not heavy. She lifted it until it rested like the lid of a box against the end of the dressing table. She leaned, peering down.

It was like looking down into a well that was a little more than three feet square. A draft carried a dank, moldy smell upward. She could see downward for only a short distance. A ladder with iron rungs was attached by rusty bolts to the stone wall.

She found Mimi's little flowered flashlight, but the beam was so faint that she could see only a few feet down. The ladder must go to the ground. Very likely from there a passage of some kind would lead out to the rocks by the sea.

As surely as if she had been transported back in time to that day she had wakened screaming. Gigi knew that someone had come into this room and forced her mother over the balcony railing to her death.

Richard. Richard, who just moments later had come running up from the beach. Richard, young then, agile.

It made sense. After all these years it made sense.

Ann. My mother. You loved me. You did not choose to leave me.

A powerful certainty moved through the girl. She had found more than just a way out of this house. She had found her whole self, which something—love, perhaps— had seen her through all the years.

Almost calm, feeling strong, Gigi started to climb down the ladder into the dark hole.

20

The iron rungs were further apart than those on an ordinary ladder. Blisters of rust came off in sharp scales on her hands. Some of the rungs were bent out of shape, so that at times her rubber soles slipped alarmingly as she lowered her weight. She gripped tightly, not letting go until she was sure each rung beneath her was solid.

From time to time she would stop, hooking an arm around a rung to get the flashlight from her pocket and direct the flickering beam downward. She hoped the battery would last until she reached the bottom.

How far down was it to the bottom? Far enough so that she knew she could be killed if she fell. What if she were descending into a well? It wasn't likely. Last night's intruder had come up this shaft somehow.

The rough stone walls, not whitewashed, smelled of moldering earth and something else—mice, rats? Might there be centepedes, tarantulas, or other crawly creatures of which she had such horror? She had no time for panic.

That door upstairs—had she locked it after her foolish attempt to pry with the knife? She must not wonder. Must not even let herself be tempted to go back up to get her billfold and passport, until now forgotten. If she could find a way out when she reached the bottom, nothing on earth would induce her to go back again up this terrible ladder.

How many rungs? She had kept no count, but it seemed as if there had been a hundred, and the wrist she had sprained was throbbing before the feeble gleam showed her there was solid stone below, not water. But she could hear water, an unhurried rushing, an intermittent slapping.

The shaft widened as she reached the last few rungs. The Stygian blackness had thinned a little. Light, very dim, was coming from somewhere.

When she put her feet on the solid stone she was trembling and weak. She was in a tiny room. Her eyes were drawn to the light. It gleamed, an irregular crevice of daylight at one end of a passageway, a tunnel, which slanted downward and looked as if it had been hewn from the living rock. She could hear the sea more plainly now, the waves washing against the rocks.

And she could see that water covered the floor at the other end of the tunnel. It crossed her mind that there might be another passageway to the cellars of the house, perhaps through the ancient, rotting wood that buttressed one side of this little room. The light, as she flashed it around briefly, showed no sign of a door, but it caught the glint of two bright eyes on a ledge halfway up. A rat. More bright eyes. Slipping, stumbling, on the downward slant of the wet, uneven stones, she half ran toward the daylight at the other end.

The water sloshed over her sneakers. It came to her knees. She steadied herself with one hand on the slimy rocks of the wall. In places the passage widened until it seemed to be a natural cave, a perfect hideout for smugglers, one which at any other time might have been interesting to explore. But a chest spilling with jewels would not have tempted her now. It was life that was precious.

The crash of the surf was louder. Her eyes on the irregular opening, she could see sky, the glint of sun on bright water. The water had reached her waist and waves had dashed repeatedly in her face by the time she emerged from the narrow cleft in the rocks.

Soaked, even to her hair, water pouring off her, she dragged herself up to a rock that was above the reach of the waves and wide enough to stand on in the gloriously open world of sea birds and sun and fresh air.

There was no beach here below her; the rocks plunged straight down. A glance showed her that even the few feet of distance made the crevice where she had emerged hard to distinguish. She was glad she would never have to find it again. All she had to do now was to clamber up over these rocks and get away.

Crouching low, she climbed to a vantage point from which she could peer through the rocks and see around to the back of the house. As she had expected, the truck was not there. Concepción had not been gone for an hour yet, and if she had gone to the market in Palma, as Richard said she did on Saturdays, it would be a long time before she could come back. It seemed safe enough to assume that Richard would not come back so early in the day.

The wind was sharp in spite of the bright sun. Her thin clothes clung to her wetly. Although she had a horror of going back into that house, it would surely be stupid not to take a few minutes to get dry clothes, her passport, ticket, and billfold from her room. She could spare another minute for a dash into the kitchen to get some food. She was weak from hunger.

And she should see Mimi. Mimi must have wondered, if she'd had lucid moments, why she hadn't returned to that upstairs room since night before last. She might even, through the boarded windows, have heard her hoarse screaming off and on all day yesterday. If she could just see her for a couple of minutes, long enough to reassure her, manage to communicate something without alarming her . . .

What would reassure her? Gigi knew it wouldn't matter much what she said to the dulled, dying mind of the grandmother who, in health and her most lucid moments, had believed that every cloud had a silver lining.

She hauled herself up over the remaining rocks and ran across the driveway toward the front of the house. She knew she was taking a chance, but she couldn't believe it was too much of a chance. The truck that Concepción was driving made quite a bit of noise. If she should hear it coming, she knew she could hide somewhere in that big house and get out again. Concepción wouldn't be likely to do any checking to see if she was still in her room. The slight risk was well worth taking.

Her skin was cold all over, but inside her was a surging of warmth from the exercise and glorious feeling of free- · dom. She pulled open the heavy door of the *entrada*, bright with its fountain and plants and gleaming tiles, and ran up the staircase.

As she opened the door to the salon, dark, the curtains not yet drawn open to the day, the lingering smell of breakfast bacon lured her toward the kitchen. Surely it was sensible to snatch some sort of food to provide the strength and energy she would need for these next few hours.

A roll, dry and cold. Delicious. She stripped a banana and crammed it into her mouth. Brown-spotted, too ripe, it was ambrosia. Even the skin would probably have tasted good, she thought as she tossed it into the trash basket.

A quick look into the refrigerator revealed almost bare shelves, proof that supplies were needed. A lone tomato, red-ripe but firm. She put it in her hip pocket. A small wrapped package held a white substance that looked like lard. Cheese. She took a hungry bite of it and put the rest of it in her other hip pocket. Then she hurried out through the salon again, up the balcony stairs, and opened the door on the right.

Mimi's door might be locked. That thought didn't occur to Gigi until she was almost at the top of the dark stairs. But surely Concepción wouldn't have felt a need to lock it, with that bolt on the tower room so firmly pushed into place. She was right. The knob turned easily, not locked. Gigi felt almost clever to think that she was so successfully outwitting the two who had plotted against her.

She entered the room, stiflingly warm and dimly lighted as it had been before. The bedside light showed Mimi sitting propped against pillows, a breakfast tray over her knees.

Mimi's eyes were open, staring, a look of surprise on the wasted face. But the look of surprise was not for Gigi. The dull, staring eyes did not see her.

With a little cry, the girl ran toward the bed. She caught hold of a bony, cool hand. Orange juice had spilled from a tipped glass, run into the lace of her bed jacket and down over a scattering of capsules and the tangled rosary. Eyes still staring, she slumped sideways.

She was dead.

21

GO *to your room. Get passport, billfold, airline ticket.*
Again Gigi began obeying instructions, her shocked
mind not able to clear itself of the surprised look on that
dead face. Had Mimi not guessed she was dying? Had she
really thought that there would be another spring?

As she went down the balcony steps into the big dark
room, she wiped blurred eyes on a sleeve that was still wet
with salt water. No time for tears or shock. Just grab the
things she had to have, a jacket, no time for changing.

No time for anything. A sound behind her. The front
door was opening. "Gigi?"

She froze, turned slowly. Richard was coming in the

front door. He wore a cheerful red sports coat. In the dimness she saw him set his suitcase down.

She said something. Maybe hello. Her mind failed her, did not tell her what to do now.

Richard was crossing to the windows to pull back the draperies, let the sun come in, throw light on her face. She wondered what it held. What it should hold.

He was coming toward her. "Where has Concepción gone? I noticed that the truck is missing."

"Oh. Is it? The market, I guess. You did say, I think, that she went to the market in Palma on Saturdays . . ."

"Or to Sóller. Yes. This is Saturday, isn't it? Right. But I would hardly have thought— Never mind." He gave her one of his nice smiles. "I'm back a little early. Well. Fill me in. You've managed?"

"Yes." She ran her tongue over dry lips, tried to return his smile, tried to stop shaking.

"Not too bored?" If he were surprised to see her still alive, his face gave no more hint than the face of any disciplined actor on the stage when a sudden mishap necessitated improvisation of lines.

"Not too bored."

He came closer, his eyes sharpening. "You're wet. My word, child, look at you. Even your hair. Don't tell me that you've had yourself another cold dip?"

"I . . ." Gigi's hands fumbled to her hair. As she pushed it back from her forehead she wondered if there might still be smudges of rust on her hands from the ladder to leave telltale marks. "I went for a walk on the beach. Slipped off a rock, fell." She rubbed her palms on the back of her jeans, felt the bulging pockets that held Mimi's flashlight, the food. "You know me . . ." She forced a laugh which ended on a note of hysteria. She tried to cover with a cough. "Clumsy me."

"I don't think you're so clumsy. I would say that you are rather a graceful, quite well-coordinated young lady." His dark eyes stayed on her face, probing blackly.

"Richard, I think I'll go back."

He frowned and smiled at the same time. "You can't mean back to the States, surely?"

"Yes. I don't feel right about staying on here."

"My dear child, you've very welcome." He moved his hands in a wide inclusive gesture. "*Mi casa es su casa.*"

It was indeed her house.

"It has been dull for you, I know. But I have all sorts of lovely plans for you."

"I know. I'm sure."

Lovely plans. She tried to think of words that would make sense, not reveal that she was aware of all his plans for her. "I don't feel that I belong in this house. Ca'n Cornitx . . . it's lovely, but now it doesn't interest me." Manners, remember manners. Try to sound like something out of Amy Vanderbilt.

"Doesn't interest you?" His smile was the same—gentle, sweet, but it chilled her.

She faltered. "All I am trying to say is that the house is yours. Of course. Quite rightly. I wouldn't have it any other way. I mean, a big, old ruin like this—I don't need to complicate my life." Don't overdo it, you fool. "You've been awfully kind, but . . ."

"But . . . ?" He said it smoothly, his eyes penetrating, guessing too much.

Unnerved by his scrutiny, she laughed a little wildly, then tried to tone it down as she said, hoping her words would seem only like an impulsive burst of candor, "What I really mean is that I don't like it here. Much. Not any." She improvised, without hope. "This house has . . . I think it's haunted."

"I told you that." The smile was gone. Deep in the darkness of his eyes she saw the ghosts of Ca'n Cornitx. They hovered, thirsty for new blood to replace that which flowed in the pictures on the walls. Warm, wet, young, it would keep them alive.

She pushed again with unsteady fingers at her damp hair. "As soon as I can get myself looking decent, I would like to go. I was on my way upstairs to pack. There is an afternoon plane, and if I hurry, I can make it. I wouldn't think of asking you to drive me to Palma, since you just got back, but if you could just take me to some place where I can get a taxi—Son Baraitx? Mimi said once that everybody uses taxis here . . . not expensive . . . and . . ." She was gibbering, had to stop it.

"I'll drive you to Palma. You're hurting my feelings, leaving so soon, but I'm trying to put myself in your place, trying to understand." He lit a cigarette. The star ruby on his little finger winked in the light.

He was trying to understand. Gigi saw that plainly. She was sure that no message had come summoning him to Almeria, but she was equally sure that he had gone there, establishing an alibi while Concepción, poor fool, had been left here to do the dirty work. He must wonder what had gone wrong. For the moment he was pretending that he would let her go. He would keep up that pretense until he could plan again.

"So"—she bared her teeth in what she hoped was a reasonable imitation of a smile—"I'll just go on up now. It will take an hour, at least. I'll need to bathe, pack. What time is it now?" She looked at her watch. It had been stopped by the immersion in the water. "This crazy watch . . ."

He glanced at the big clock. "It's just a couple of minutes past eleven."

"Oh, fine. I can be ready in an hour." She backed away from him, had to back away because of the bulge of the flashlight and the food in her pockets.

"Shall you want lunch before you go?"

"Oh, no. I'm not at all hungry. Thanks very much. You eat something, though. And then we'll go."

"Yes, then we'll go. Why are you so nervous? Has something happened?"

"Happened? Oh, no." She widened her eyes, making them round. She had reached the door. *Please, God, let me get away from him now, get up to my room. Give me that hour. Let me climb down the ladder again. That blessed ladder, past the rats or scorpions or snakes.* No longer was she afraid of things that crawled.

She opened the door, ran along the passage, across the hollow square of the courtyard, up the zigzagging steps. Up at the door of her room, panting as she slid back the bolt, she had a heart-stopping moment of wondering what she would do if the door were locked from the inside. Once, an eon ago, she had hoped she had locked it.

It opened. Thank God she had forgotten to lock it.

With fingers that shook, she extracted her wallet, passport, airline ticket from her purse, stuffing them down inside her shirt. She snatched up a jacket, put it on.

A noise. The chug, chug of a motor coming up the hill. She rushed to the back window to look out. The truck was stopping out in back. Richard came out to meet Concepción.

"Concepción, where in hell have you been? *Por qué*

no . . .?" A torrent of words followed as Concepción climbed down from the truck. She kept trying to interrupt him.

"*Vaca!* You stupid cow!" His fist struck a savage blow across the woman's face. Concepción staggered backward against the truck, cans and vegetables rolling from the fallen basket.

The words went on, but Gigi waited to hear no more. Her hour had been snatched from her. She had minutes now, not that precious hour which she had counted on to get away from this house.

The hole in the closet floor yawned black. She sat on the floor, then slid her feet to search for the rungs that might still take her down to safety.

She must be quick, hurry, not like on that first, hesitant descent when she had paused to flash the beam over what lay below. She knew now what was there. She could not linger to face the sort of death Richard would devise. He had to kill her. Yes, now that he had talked to Concepción, he would have to kill her.

Her breath came in loud gasps. The little flashlight slipped from her back pocket. She heard it hit the stone floor far below. As her feet scraped the rungs she listened, but not pausing, for sounds that might come any minute from above?

Why, oh, why hadn't she had brains enough to lock the door this time? In her terror at hearing the truck and those few words, she had completely forgotten to do the one thing that would have given her a few precious minutes.

Her feet continued downward with no searching for safe footholds. She hadn't the courage to go back up, important though that might be. Richard, she hoped, might take a little while to plan his next strategy. He might even wait for that whole hour she had told him it would take her to pack.

Unlikely.

She wondered if his stiff knee would allow him to climb down the ladder. She did not think it would. She might find him waiting for her on the rocks at the end of the tunnel.

The sounds of the sea came clearly now as she made it to the stone floor. A squeaking noise—bats, rats? It was so dark. If the little flashlight still worked at all, it might be some protection. She might even be able to use it as a weapon. She knelt, both hands feeling about for it on the dark floor.

Not dark. A pencil of slanting light. She looked up to see that the light came from a crack in the wall. It widened with the groaning and screeching of old wood, old hinges.

Fingers became visible as the crack widened—a hand, a ring set with a star ruby. A shirt cuff, white, the red sleeve of a sports coat. She saw Richard's face. He was smiling. He carried an electric lantern. Before the bright light fell full on her face, before he closed the door, she could see the great casks of the wine cellar behind him.

22

Gigi was on her feet, pressing back against the wall. Richard set the lantern on the ledge where she had seen the rat.

As if cast for the moment in the role of guide escorting a party of tourists, he said, "Now, this door opens into one end of the wine cellar. The door—together with that ladder leading upward—was discovered at the time that the present owner purchased the house. Back in the early days of intrigue and skulduggery, when no one could be trusted, not even the pretty visitors from faraway lands, it was found necessary sometimes for the lord of the manor to take the law into his own hands in order to protect his interests."

He brushed cobwebs fastidiously from his red coat. "Are you following me, pretty visitor? Just practicing, of course. Just wanting to find out if you think I could get a job as a tour guide escorting stupid Americans through moldering castles."

"Stupid . . ." Gigi said the word dully.

"Quite. Afraid I must agree there."

"You can have the house." Gigi took a step toward him, her hands outstretched.

"Don't come any closer." He took a gun from his pocket. "Concepción told me just now—among other things— about your handy little karate chop to her throat. I'm no match for your physical skills—more's the pity. Mimi took care of that years ago, and I've never forgiven her. I always knew that the day would come when I could get even. It seemed worthwhile hanging on. Frightful bore, all these years, but there have been a few small dividends along the way."

She looked into the dead depths of his dark eyes. "You are like I was—" She stopped. "No, like I thought I was."

"Make sense, if it is not too much of an effort."

"If a child has no one to love him, he dies. Emotionally. You died, Richard."

"Did I? Splendid. You are rather hooked on that pretty concept, aren't you? It may be true. A conscience would be such a nuisance. I'll have none about you."

"No more than you've had . . . than you've had about my mother."

"Oh, right-o. You have, I suppose, remembered? Or perhaps just put two and two together? Pity that's it's come too late to do you any good."

"Why did you kill her?"

"She made it necessary. As you have done. Poked her

nose into all sorts of things that were none of her business, and found some financial matters that might have ruined me, might have meant prison, even. She threatened me. Not very clever of her. But she was more clever than you, I'll give her that much. She would never, for instance, have believed that was Mimi's grave. She would have had brains enough to have known that they would never have allowed a pagan Protestant to be buried in a Catholic cemetery."

"Whose grave . . . ?" The words were hollow, amplified by the stone walls.

"Good God! Who cares?" He picked another cobweb from his sleeve and shrugged. "Some poor bastard died. Providence provides these small breaks even to sinners from time to time. I'm not one to question Providence. I simply take advantage of it."

"It was Carlos's grave—Octavia Milton's gardener's grave!"

Surprise replaced the look of arrogance on the handsome face.

"I spent an afternoon in Son Baraitx. That's something you didn't know, something even Concepción didn't know because by then she had started drinking. Or did you know that she drinks?" She lifted her chin and tried to sound brave and scornful. "I'll tell you something else you don't know. I called Josh Lincoln from Son Baraitx. I told him to come. He is coming."

"Lovely. Within the hour I hope, for your sake." And then calmly, "I can tell by your face that you are lying. Even if it should be true and the dear boy should arrive, I am marvelous at improvisation. I shall weep for you."

She knew that he would. Convincingly. She knew that the man she faced was an egomaniac, blinding himself to the possibility of failure. A very short distance lay between them. If she made a lunge for him, caught him off guard, threw him off balance . . . But the gun was aimed at her chest. Even karate experts did not quarrel with guns. Her mouth dry, Gigi said, "Richard, you can have this house."

"Naturally. By the terms of the will— Oh, yes, there is a will."

"That's something else that I know! I have to die before Mimi dies, but now—"

"Predecease is the word. A lovely word. Until I thought of it only a fortnight or so ago, I was in despair. I thought I should lose Ca'n Cornitx. But the lawyer Azcona, such an honorable slob, agreed that it was a sensible provision to add, so he came up here on the trot and now the document reposes in a bank vault, all tidy and legal. Everything has gone as planned. You came at my bidding, fortunately before there was any chance for you to be hypnotized again and remember some things that might have been a bit sticky for me. And now you will die before Mimi does."

Harshly, Gigi said, "I won't. I can't."

"What do you mean won't, can't . . . ?"

"She is already dead!"

"I told you that, yes, and you fell for it." The look of arrogance again. "She is dying, but not dead. Concepción told me she took her breakfast up to her this morning. She has only a few more weeks, perhaps only days, but—"

"She is dead—dead now! I saw her. I touched her!" Gigi shouted the words above the sounds of the water.

His composure seemed to waver.

"Go and see! Concepción will have found her by now!"

His dark eyes narrowed. "You are lying again."

"I am not lying. You have lost!" Gigi's laugh was high, hysterical. Frightened though she was, she pushed the momentary advantage. "Your whole wild scheme has fallen through! I haven't predeceased her, and I can't just—just disappear. You've got to prove . . ."

"Dear me. So now you think you have me, is that it? You have already disappeared."

"Concepción . . ." She remembered his fist smashing across the woman's face. "Do you think now that Concepción will . . ."

"She will do what I tell her to do. Say what I tell her to say. A role in a film is her price. She deludes herself into thinking she'll have a career."

"Even if she's willing to lie, you would not dare to shoot me."

"What do you think this gun is for? I intend to kill you."

"And if they find me with a bullet hole, don't you think they will suspect you?"

"Ah, but they won't find you. Not in any condition for tests to be made. I have researched the plausibility of too many scripts not to know what one can and cannot get away with. Up to now this script has been rather hackneyed —the tired old ploy about the brash young girl and the secret passage. Incidentally, I've been the only one who has known about that shaft between the walls. I discovered it when I was doing the work up there. I substituted a creaky old trap door with one of my own devising. I can do anything. But nothing quite so intrigues me as to bring the hero—in this case, myself—up to an impasse and having to resolve the plot in a believable, seemingly natural way. Providence"—he made an amused gesture of crossing himself—"again provides the way. Once again I simply take advantage of what is at hand. There are sharks in these waters. They don't leave much. I should imagine some remnants of those hideous clothes you're wearing may be cast up somewhere along the shore."

Despairingly, Gigi knew his cold brain could visualize a zoom lens focusing down with as little emotion as if he were planning it for one of his films.

"And you think there won't be an investigation?"

"Oh, yes. But let's leave the details to me, shall we? I thrive on problems. Spanish law is thorough, but the advantages tend to be on the side of the Spanish citizen—which I am, as I told you. With some of the most responsible citizens on this island to vouch for my character."

She heard the click of the safety catch. The sound of the waters seemed to lessen for a few seconds. She knew she had come close to fainting. Were there other words she could say? Was there anything at all she could do?

"I do fancy the sound of my own voice—the frustrated actor in me—but it bores me now to prolong this. It's quite cold and damp here and my knee is beginning to give me a bad time. I rather wish I did not have to do this, but even you must understand that I cannot let you go."

Gigi said through stiff lips, "I'll do anything . . . promise anything . . ."

"I can't imagine anything you could offer that would interest me. Your mother—I just remembered, and it embarrasses me to recount such an old cliché—offered me her body before she 'fell' from the balcony."

The girl made a choked sound.

"Yes. She dropped her superior scorn of me and I'm afraid got a bit maudlin there toward the end about her poor orphaned child. True, I had made advances previously which—give me my due—I have never made toward you. You're not my type, though I imagine you'd not be half bad in a proper bed. Mimi has told me you were a bit free with your favors there for a while. Amusing, really, that one with her past should even bother to comment on the morals of another. I've never been judgmental, never have had sexual scruples. Part of my emotional death, as you would say." He inclined his head toward the end of the tunnel. "There is water there, as you must have discovered when you went through it a little while ago."

Gigi turned to look where the gleam from the narrow opening was reflected on the water, which she knew was waist-deep.

"I have my little idiosyncrasies. I am squeamish about blood. The thought of simply shooting you at close range makes me more than a little bit queasy. But more practically, I don't want blood spattered all over these stones, to be scraped up and analyzed later, in case they find this place. You are to go now along that passage. And when you reach the water—It's a sporting chance. You might even make it."

"I could never . . . you know I could never . . ."

"Oh, the game is fixed, rather. But I might miss. You might even make it. I should think you'd prefer that chance to just standing there gawking like a moronic child, waiting."

She crossed her arms over her chest to try to stop her convulsive shaking. She raised her eyes.

He said impatiently, "I like that look even less, as if you imagine yourself to be a saint looking imploringly upward toward heaven."

She kept her eyes turned upward, trying to freeze her face to blankness. A movement up there on the iron rungs had caught her eye. No sound was audible above the reverberating murmur of the sea. Out of the range of Richard's vision, she had glimpsed a chukka boot.

"Move!" Richard flourished the gun as he shouted the word.

Gigi did not move. The figure on the ladder moved, leaped down and sprang across the intervening space, catching Richard off balance, knocking the hand that held the gun upward. A shot. A crimson gush of blood pouring from his torn throat.

Gigi turned away from the shocked, open mouth. She groped for the ladder, feeling sick.

Josh Lincoln took her hands. She felt blood, warm and slick, against her fingers as she clung.

"Don't pass out. Gigi, are you going to pass out? I can never carry you back up that ladder."

23

G*igi* pointed toward the door. Josh pushed the life-less body aside, opened the door. They made their way through the cobwebbed wine cellar, through the laundry, where Josh's hands left bloody marks on the hanging sheets as he held them for her to pass. Upstairs, disoriented, Gigi led him along a passage that opened into the kitchen.

Concepción stood there. On the table was Mimi's breakfast tray, as if it had just been set down. The woman was holding her white apron to her mouth. Her eyes were wide, one of them purpling from Richard's blow.

Josh said, "Thank you."

The words seemed stupid to Gigi. She started to go on through the kitchen. Josh caught her arm. "I had a taxi driver bring me up here. I told him to wait. How do I tell her to send him for the police?"

Gigi looked into Concepción's frightened eyes. "*Digalo . . . el señor del taxi. La policía . . .*"

"*Mi señora es . . .*"

"*Sí. Sí, y el señor Don Ricardo también* is dead—*es muerto.*"

Concepción stared, turned then to rush out the back door. Gigi wondered if she would ever see her again.

She led Josh through the kitchen, through the salon, the passage and courtyard that led to the zigzagging stairway.

"Forty-eight steps." She sagged against him.

Josh's arm went around her, supporting her. She went into the room she had thought never to enter again and fell backward on the bed. A lump, uncomfortable, in her hip pocket. Cheese. She took it out. In her other pocket, the tomato. She looked at it, oozing red. Feeling nauseated, she dropped it, lay back again and closed her eyes.

When Josh had washed the blood from his hands in the bathroom, he came to sit on the side of the bed. He had a warm, wet washcloth and he moved it over Gigi's face and hands as if she were a little baby.

"Josh . . . how?"

His dark hair had fallen over his eyes. He pushed it back. "First—let me think what came first—the uneasiness, the gut feeling that I should not have let you go alone. I had crazy thoughts. Like maybe your grandmother wasn't even sick and the cable had been sent by somebody else just to get you there."

"Partly right."

"And then your telephone call—you remember that you told me not to come. That same afternoon the jeweler phoned me to say that the ring I had left with him was a fake. I could not believe that your grandmother would have sent you a hunk of glass. I thought, What if somebody had made the substitution without her knowing it? I thought, What if this guy, this lover, this Richard, had been the one who made the substitution—perhaps, over the years, had made others?"

Gigi was nodding as she remembered Richard's words: *There have been a few small dividends.* "So that's why you came. You are brilliant."

"No, that's not why I came. And if I'd been brilliant, I would have left right then. I wasted a whole day. And then it hit me. Richard was his name. What is a common nickname for Richard?"

"Dick—Dickie. He said I used to call him Dickie."

"I'll bet he did. But I'll bet you didn't. Rich is another nickname for Richard. I checked with Max and Carol and they agreed with what I was sure I remembered. When you were a little girl, as we saw you taken back under hypnosis, you couldn't say your r's. You said 'wed dwess.' You said 'Cwistmas twee.' You would have said 'Witch' for 'Rich.' I took the next plane."

He caught her close and kissed her and kissed her. She cried then, sobbed, clutched him, hanging onto the first reality she had known in many days.

But there was a dead man down at the bottom of the shaft.

Gigi got off the bed. She went to look out the window, wondering how long it would take for the police to come. "Josh, why did you say thank you to Concepción?"

He was standing behind her. "We owe her your life. She showed me where your room was. I came up here and saw that God-awful hole. I heard enough on the way down to know I had to be careful or you'd be killed."

His arms were about her. She leaned back. Her eyes on the sea, she said, "Majorca at almond blossom time is like a basket of flowers floating on the sea."

"What's that got to do with anything?"

"Richard said that." She sighed. "There is so much you don't know. It will take a long, long time to tell you everything."

"We'll have the time."

24

Gigi had brought balloons, a big bouquet of them, which now floated above the flowers on a grave in a Protestant cemetery in Palma. They danced gaily in the soft, warm breeze, all in the bright pastel colors Mimi had loved.

Gigi wore a yellow dress that Mimi would have liked, almost a match for her hair. She clung to Josh Lincoln's hand, aware of the strength that had seen her through the last twenty-four hours of police and questioning. Unknown friends had produced an American consul, who had moved through it all, facilitating, translating, explaining finally that the necessary hearing would be only a formality.

This was a formality, these words said by a stranger in a

clerical collar, praying now. Gigi tried to take comfort. The words were in English, but she did not try to understand their meaning. Some day, maybe. Never, maybe. But she felt a need to believe from now on in things she could not understand. Josh would help her. She was ready for total commitment.

She lifted her head. Shook hands with the clergyman, thanked him.

Octavia Milton had been there, together with a number of persons whose names Gigi had not even heard. Concepción had been there, but now she was leaving.

They turned to leave too, walking under blossoms that said it was spring. Josh said, "I never saw balloons on a grave before. You didn't tell me why you wanted them. Is that a Spanish custom?"

Gigi glanced back at the colors dancing happily, carefree, childlike above the grave. "No," she said. "Just Mimi."

About the Author

In 1970 NAOMI A. HINTZE received an
Edgar Allan Poe Special Award for her first novel,
You'll Like My Mother. This book was made into
a movie in 1972. *Aloha Means Goodbye* will be
filmed in 1974. Three of her books,
You'll Like My Mother, Aloha Means Goodbye and
Listen, Please Listen, have been Book-of-the-Month
Club Alternates. Mrs. Hintze lives in
Charlottesville, Virginia, in a wonderful modern
house. She travels throughout the world,
frequently to Majorca, the setting of *Cry Witch*.